The Gift Exchange

&You Anthologies

Another Chance to Get It Right: A New Year's Eve Anthology

As the Snow Drifts: A Cozy Winter Anthology

Craving You: A Spicy Valentine's Day Anthology

Recipes for Romance: A Sweet Valentine's Day Anthology

Just One . . .: A Summer Romance Anthology

Not As It Seems: A Gothic Anthology

The Gift Exchange

A Young Adult Holiday Anthology

Edited & Arranged by

Nicole Frail

And You Press
an imprint of Nicole Frail Books, LLC
www.andyoupress.com

Contents

Lauren is haunted by the memory of last Christmas, when she gave her boyfriend a funny T-shirt, and he broke up with her, saying she was obviously not serious about their relationship. This year, Lauren is dating Ian, and she is determined to find an impressive, grown-up gift to prove her feelings for him are real.

When Adriana gets a personalized Secret Santa gift from Liam (the co-worker she knows has a crush on her), it accidentally triggers a wild chase involving government agents and a mistaken identity. What starts as a sweet gesture spirals into a harrowing misadventure that brings these two teens into close contact that might just spark a Christmas romance.

Sometimes being fourteen years old is tough. But between a sweet kitten and a bit of hope found on a star-filled night, JoAnna just might have the best holiday ever.

Introduction
Nicole Frail, Publisher & Editor

Young adult fiction books have always been among my favorites to read, edit, and publish. Despite being "kids," the characters in young adult fiction are quite complex.

The main characters in this category are often in love for the first time; they're dealing with issues at home and in school; they're questioning the loyalty of their friends; they're wanting to live BIG even when their world may feel quite small. And they have their whole lives ahead of them to figure out.

Of course, we, as readers, see only a snippet of their lives, and whether we're adults reading YA (#ireadya) or part of the intended audience of middle and high school students, we can relate to their journeys. We either remember what it feels like to be a teen, or we currently *are* teens and we're right there with them through those first kisses and crushes, betrayals and hard losses.

The teens in The Gift Exchange have been challenged in one way or the other by the holiday season and the task of finding and giving a gift to someone special in their lives. On top of everything else going on in their lives, here comes the stress of the holidays—and we're here for it. We'll cheer them on, we'll sigh and swoon, and sometimes we'll sympathize. (All perfectly acceptable behaviors during the season of giving!)

I hope you enjoy this collection of young adult short stories. It's the first for this age range for And You Press/Nicole Frail Books, and hopefully not the last!

The Gift of Christmas Present

The Gift of Christmas Present

Katie Fitzgerald

"Last Christmas, I gave you a shirt." Waving an ornament, Lauren's younger sister Chloe danced around the pre-lit tree, butchering a holiday pop classic. "But the very next day, you sent me away."

"Will you stop already?" Lauren had been hearing this version of Wham! all afternoon, and Chloe had yet to get the reaction she was hoping for, but a girl could only take so much. Middle school humor was bad enough when it wasn't personal, but these song lyrics were a dig at Lauren's dating history.

"What? I'm just singing the truth. You gave Ben a shirt for Christmas, and he dumped you."

Lauren opened her mouth to protest but shut it again instantly. Not only was it stupid to care what had happened with her old boyfriend when she was happily dating Ian, but Chloe was also pretty much right.

When she and Ben had exchanged gifts after the choir concert last December, Lauren had been so excited to give him the perfect gift she'd found online. When they had started dating over the summer, one of their favorite things to do was drive through the ice cream shop, then ride around their small town licking their cones and singing along to the radio. When Lauren saw the ad for the "Scoop, there it is" T-shirt on social media, she knew instantly that it would make Ben laugh. Since Ben's laugh was one of her favorite things, this felt like a no-brainer. She had pressed the Order button and gone to bed that night bursting with Christmas cheer.

Two weeks later, when Ben opened the wrapped package, the laughter that came out wasn't the pleasant sound Lauren had heard in the car all summer, but a surprised, almost disdainful grunt. Then he'd said, "Oh. This is the actual gift. Wow. Um, thanks."

Seeming like he wanted to be anywhere else, he'd handed Lauren the small, sparkly bag containing his gift for her. The contents of the little red jeweler's box inside made her gasp. It was a beautiful necklace, a gold heart on a chain, and it looked like it cost a lot more than she'd spent on that silly shirt.

Despite not really being a jewelry girl, Lauren wore that necklace every day until the new year, but Ben never wore the shirt. When they went back to school at the end of break, he'd taken her aside before the homeroom bell.

As part of his break-up speech, he'd told her: "And honestly, it was pretty clear from your gift that we're not on the same page. As my mom said, that's a gift you give your brother, not a serious boyfriend." And that was the end of that.

"I hope you're planning to do a better job shopping for Ian," Chloe now warned as she hung her ornament and went to the box for another.

Lauren was already one step ahead of her sister. Scrolling through her texts, she revisited the one she had received from Ian last night. *Presents after school Friday?*

Underneath it was her response, bookended by smiling emojis presenting a holiday joy she did not feel. *Sure! Can't wait.*

Tomorrow was Monday. In the next four days, Lauren had one mission: to choose a Christmas present so undeniably perfect, Ian would never question how she felt about him.

The next day at lunch, Lauren went into full girl-detective mode, analyzing everything Ian was carrying, wearing, and talking about for clues to what he wanted for Christmas. Unfortunately, everything struck her as being in the same category as a T-shirt. He loved baseball caps, but he already had so many, and the odds of her choosing something he already had were high. He was walking around with a portrait he had done in art class, which he needed to put in his locker, and that made Lauren briefly consider art supplies, but then she remembered that's what her aunt usually gave her for her birthday. Auntie vibes were not what she was going for.

"I'm thinking about your Christmas present," she told him as they walked to the trash can to deposit their garbage. "Want to guess what it could be?" If he threw out some guesses, that would tell her what he really wanted, and then she could just go get one of those things.

But Ian kissed her cheek and said, "And ruin the surprise? No way! Christmas presents are sacred. You can't just go blabbing about them ahead of time." He lowered his voice to a stage whisper. "What would Santa think?"

Lauren laughed. She pressed him just once more. "Well, what do you hope it is, then?"

Ian gave her that warm grin that had won her over so easily at the back-to-school dance and said, "I hope it's from you. That's all. You're amazing, and you'll come up with something amazing."

I won't, though, Lauren thought. Instead of Wham!, a different pop hit from the eighties ran through her mind, ending with that lyric about spending Christmas by herself this year. She sighed. This was impossible.

That night, she scrolled endlessly through website after website, adding to her cart all the things that made her think of Ian: Mario Kart merch, an Eagles poster, a boxed set of dragon fantasy novels, bright-green earbuds, soccer stuff. A couple times she almost added a T-shirt or mug with a funny phrase, but then she realized she was backsliding into her old ways, and she deleted those. Then she deleted the contents of every cart, slammed down the laptop lid, and flopped onto her bed.

During study hall the next day, Ian was at a band lesson, so Lauren was left with Troy, Ian's best friend, for company. Mr. Haynes didn't care if they talked as long as they kept their voices at a reasonable volume, so Lauren seized the opportunity.

"What are you getting Ian for Christmas?"

Troy gave her a weird look. "Nothing, I guess? We don't really do gifts. Unless you count, like, video game gift cards. Why? Are you worried we'll get him the same thing? That seems unlikely."

Lauren rolled her eyes. "No, I'm just . . . brainstorming. Does he ever wear jewelry?"

Troy's brow furrowed deeper. "Not that I can remember in my entire life."

"But what if he dressed up, or went to a wedding or something?"

"I've never seen him dressed up. Are you guys going to a wedding?"

Lauren sighed. She was trying to understand what the male equivalent of the necklace Ben had given her would be so she could try to find it for Ian, but Troy was no help. "No, but I'm trying to think of a nice present. A serious one."

"For Ian? Why? All you guys do together is laugh. Trust me, he likes that. Don't mess with it."

"But this is a *Christmas* present," Lauren said, as though Troy was deliberately misunderstanding her. "It should be special."

"Did you ask him what he wants?" Troy got out a notebook, clearly planning to do homework to get out of this conversation.

"He said whatever I get will be amazing."

"Well, there you go, then." Then he popped in earbuds and started working on his trig.

Lauren took out her phone, wishing it was possible to Google personalized information. *What's a good gift to show Ian I'm serious about our relationship?* Her phone didn't have the answer, but it did have some new texts. One was Ian saying he couldn't wait to kiss her goodbye at his locker after the last bell. That one made her smile. Another was her mom reminding her that she would be home later than usual because she was taking Chloe to the dentist. And the last one was from Ella, Lauren's newest friend, inviting her to bake cookies after school. The perfect distraction.

I'm in, Lauren replied.

"So, have you guys exchanged gifts yet?" Ella asked while the first batch of miniature shortbread trees was baking. "Palmer wants to wait until Friday, but the suspense is killing me!"

"We're doing Friday, too," Lauren said. "But I don't actually have a gift yet."

Ella gave her a thoughtful look. "Really? Well, you'd better hurry up. It's probably too late to have something shipped."

"Tell me about it," Lauren said. "But everything just feels so . . ."

"Dumb?" Ella nodded. "I know. I saw a couple reels with gift ideas for guys, and they were all about shaving and playing video games."

"Exactly!" Lauren said, glad that at least another girl understood her dilemma. "Those are gifts you could give your brother, you know?"

"Yes!" Ella agreed. "It's like if you gave your boyfriend pants or a shirt or something. So not romantic." The oven timer beeped, and she bent to remove the tray from the oven.

Lauren was glad for the blast of heat because it meant there was a reason for her face to be red besides humiliation. "Right," she said, trying to keep her tone light. "So, what are you giving Palmer?" Lauren had known Ella only a couple of months, but clearly she was extremely knowledgeable about girlfriend stuff.

"Cuff links," Ella said simply. Lauren picked up a spatula and scooped a cookie onto the cooling rack, then glanced at Ella, hoping she would explain a bit more. Lauren wasn't sure what cuff links actually were. She had always associated them with golf for some reason.

"I mean, he'll probably be prom king," Ella continued. "So he'll need them for that, and, I don't know. It just seems more mature than what other girls give."

Lauren cleared her throat, then allowed the most ridiculous lie to fall right out of her mouth. "It's funny," she said, keeping her eyes on the cookies as she spoke. "That's just what I was thinking of getting for Ian."

When Ella laughed—not mockingly, but good-naturedly, as though this coincidence was a sign of sisterhood—Lauren realized she had just come to a decision. She was going to join Ella among the ranks of good, serious girlfriends by making this lie come true.

Because of the choir concert, Lauren couldn't get to the mall on Wednesday afternoon or evening, but on Thursday, she, her mom, and Chloe took a ride over after dinner. While those two looked for a last-minute gift for Chloe's piano teacher, Lauren headed to the men's department of one of the mall's anchor stores.

She really didn't want help from a salesperson, but she also knew her mom would be in a hurry to leave once she finished her own shopping, so after a few minutes of awkward wandering, she gave in and went to the counter.

"Cuff links?" The guy behind the counter gave her a look similar to the one she'd gotten from Troy the other day, but he didn't say anything else. Instead, he led her to the store's selection, then left her there to make her own choice.

Judging from the photos on some of the packages, cuff links were worn on the cuffs of a dress shirt. Okay, well, Ella had mentioned prom. Ian would dress up for that. And maybe if he had cuff links from his girlfriend, he'd wear them to school. Who knew? They definitely had the sophisticated look she was going for, and she could just imagine his mom seeing them in his backpack and saying, "Wow, Lauren really likes you."

Not fully confident in her decision, but ready to be done, she narrowed down her choices, eliminating colors and styles until she was left with one set of moderately priced, round, green cuff links with gold trim. "I'll take these," she told the sales clerk, paid, and went off to meet her mother.

It wasn't until she smelled the hot coffee that she remembered she had not wanted to walk this way. The coffee kiosk reminded her of Ben, not just because he loved coffee, but also because he worked there. And . . . yup, there he was, handing a lady's card back to her over the garland-covered cash register and now looking right at her.

Immediately, he stepped out from behind the counter, and Lauren found herself turning her shopping bag so he'd be sure to see the logo. Ben glanced at it briefly but didn't seem to really take it in. Instead he said, "I just saw your mom go by. She went that way." He pointed toward the center of the mall.

"Yeah, she's shopping with my sister. I came to get something for Ian."

"Oh, right," Ben said. "How's that going?"

"Great!" Lauren said, and she swung the bag again, really wanting him to notice that she was giving her boyfriend a real, grown-up gift that proved she knew how to be in a relationship. But Ben was oblivious. Determined to get him to see how much she had improved since their break-up, she continued: "By the way, you can totally get rid of that shirt I gave you last year."

Ben furrowed his brow, then nodded as he understood what she meant. "Well, I already donated it to Goodwill." He looked away, then back at Lauren. "It was . . . you know, not my style."

"Oh, right. Okay." Nothing about this conversation was going the way Lauren had imagined. How was it that even after doing everything right, she still felt awkward and out of place?

Thankfully, her mom was now headed in her direction, so it would be easy to make her escape. "I really need to go," she said. "Good seeing you."

Ben raised a hand to wave goodbye. "Merry Christmas, Lauren," he said, and she hustled away from him.

"Wasn't that Ben?" Chloe asked on the way to the exit. She started humming her little song again until their mom nudged her and told her to stop.

"Everything good?" her mom asked, giving Lauren a concerned look.

Lauren called to mind the image of the fancy-looking, mildly expensive men's accessories tucked away in her bag. She considered the uncomfortable conversation she'd just had with her ex-boyfriend and how, even after making changes, she still felt insignificant and childish around him. *Was* everything good? Part of her still felt that a gift should be more personal, more specific to the recipient, and more fun than this. But Ella and Palmer seemed happy, and she knew she couldn't endure another embarrassment like the one she'd had with Ben. So, she nodded.

"Yup. Fine," she told her mom.

And if she couldn't sleep that night, she told herself it was from anticipation and not anxiety over having gotten it wrong yet again.

"I seriously cannot wait for this afternoon!" Ian said when they met in the hallway mid-morning. "I think you're going to love what I got you."

"You're like a little kid." Lauren laughed, enjoying how adorable he was when he got like this.

"And I finally get to know what you got me! And then we get to hang out during break. Seriously, this is the best day."

He still had that same goofy, childlike grin on his face when they met at the picnic table in front of the school to finally open their gifts. Ian's brown scarf brought out the creamy color of his eyes, and for a moment, Lauren just looked at him, enjoying how cute he was, and how tall, and how kind and sweet. He deserved a nice gift. So what if he hardly used it? That's what would make it special.

"Here," Ian said, presenting her with a somewhat squashed, sloppily wrapped rectangle decorated with snowflakes and glittery Santa hats. "Sorry," he said. "It's hard to find good elves to help wrap this time of year."

Lauren giggled and slowly began to unwrap her gift. Inside the paper was a white box, the kind her mom usually used when she gave people clothes. With Ian's dancing eyes looking on, Lauren slowly pulled the lid off the box. The item inside was made of blue cotton fabric, and she didn't even have it fully unfolded before Ian read the front of the shirt aloud.

"Scoop, there it is!" he said. "Get it? Because you always eat ice cream when we watch movies, and you love listening to old pop music with your mom!"

Lauren was completely stunned. Incredulous, she looked back and forth between Ian and the T-shirt lying limp in her hands on the tabletop. "I saw it at Goodwill," Ian continued. "And I just knew, instantly, it was perfect for you."

Suddenly, Lauren couldn't stop laughing. Gasping for air, she kept trying to stop and explain what was so funny, but the whole thing was just too much.

"You went to—That shirt was—" she sputtered. "I can't believe—"

"Okay," Ian said. "It's funny, but not that funny." He nudged her with his elbow. "But I'm glad you like it."

Taking a few deep breaths, Lauren said, "I'll tell you a story in a minute, but first . . . you'd better open this."

That good, hearty laugh had pulled all the nervous energy from her body, and now Lauren felt steady and calm. She handed over the little box from the mall wrapped in reindeer paper.

Ian made a big show of shaking it, trying to peek through the paper, and gently squeezing the box. Finally, with an exaggeratedly mysterious look on his face, he tore the paper to shreds, tossing it aside as he made his way toward the gift.

When Lauren saw the look on his face, she knew instinctively that she had done it again.

"Cool," Ian said, rolling the cuff links around in his palm. "Um, is this like what Ella got Palmer?" He looked over at Lauren, his expression turning thoughtful. "Sorry, but I don't actually know what they are." He held them to his ears. "Not earrings, I'm guessing."

Lauren had never felt her mood swing as violently as it had in that moment. Her laughter of moments ago was now turning to tears, and she had to blink to keep them from blotting out her vision entirely. "They're cuff links," she whispered. "Stupid cuff links."

"I don't think they're stupid," Ian said gently, clearly confused by the sudden shift in mood.

"I'm stupid," Lauren said. "I don't know what I was thinking."

"Apparently that I need to step up my wardrobe."

Ian was clearly teasing, but Lauren couldn't find her sense of humor.

"It's happening again," she said, shaking her head in disbelief. "I did it again."

"If you want me to wear them, Lauren, I will. I just have to figure out how."

Lauren took a deep breath. "I almost got you bright-green earbuds," she told him. "And a soccer sticker for your water bottle." Ian's face lit up, and Lauren inwardly kicked herself. Her instincts had been right.

"But this is also cool," Ian said, still trying to make her feel at ease.

"That shirt you got me?" Lauren said. "That's what I gave Ben last year." That exact shirt, she was pretty sure, but there was no sense in getting into that now. "And he broke up with me over it."

Ian's eyes widened. "What? Why?"

"Because I obviously wasn't that serious about our relationship," Lauren muttered. "I didn't even think about an expensive, romantic gift."

Ian started to nod, and Lauren saw realization dawn on his face. "You bought me the gift Ben would have wanted."

Lauren couldn't object. That was exactly what she had done. She had taken Ben's criticism so fully to heart that she hadn't thought about what *Ian* wanted. She had sought advice from Troy and Ella, and approval from Ben, but none of them had been able to express Lauren's feelings for Ian. Those were hers alone, and by trying to fit someone else's mold, she had been denying Ian the opportunity to receive a meaningful gift that came from her heart, instead of someone else's mind.

"You know what I like about you, Lauren?" Ian asked suddenly.

She shrugged. "Troy says it's that we laugh together."

"He's right. I love that." He reached for Lauren's hand and held it between both of his. "But it's also the way you remember all the little things about people. You know my favorite color, and my favorite book, and when I mention a song, you go listen to it, and when we have an inside joke, you keep cracking up over it for weeks and weeks. You're not like anyone else. You're different. And it's awesome."

Lauren leaned against Ian, her puffy winter coat snuggling against his leather one. "I should have gotten you a baseball cap," she said. "Or a Mario Kart shirt. I'm sorry."

"That's definitely more my thing," Ian said. "But no apology needed. The real gift is having you as my girlfriend." He gave her a noisy smack of a kiss on the top of her head and then grinned broadly.

"I know, so cheesy, but also so true."

Lauren beamed. Then she had another realization. "You know, there's one thing I could give you that no one else possibly could."

"What's that?"

Slipping her hand from between his, Lauren stroked Ian's cheek with her palm, then brought her face closer to his before pressing their chilled lips together. Tuning out any doubts that threatened to creep in, she poured her emotions into the kiss, focusing singularly on Ian and nothing else. A moment later, their lips weren't cold anymore, but plump and warm and pink as Santa's rosy cheeks.

"I definitely don't want that from anybody else," Ian said. "Just keep being Lauren, okay?" He moved a stray hair behind her ear.

With a contented sigh, she nodded. He had given her so much more than a shirt for Christmas. "Okay. I can do that."

"Then it'll be like Christmas every day," Ian said, drawing her in for another kiss.

About the Author

Katie Fitzgerald has been a featured author in three short romance collections and has published more than thirty short stories. Her short romances appear online at Spark Flash Fiction and Micromance Magazine, as well as in various anthologies. She is a 2024 Sparkie Award recipient for Best Romantic Suspense and has been nominated for the Pushcart Prize and the Cupid Prize. A graduate of Vassar College and a trained librarian, Katie resides in Maryland with her husband and five kids.

You can follow Katie on Instagram at:
@katiefitzstories

To learn more about Katie, visit her website at:
https://bio.site/katiefitzgerald

Mad-Dashing Through the Snow

Mad-Dashing Through the Snow

Justine Gunn

If someone asked me how I ended up dressed like an elf, suspended three stories above the honking traffic of a city I've never been to before, I'd give an answer that might surprise them: The Gift Exchange.

Let me rewind.

It started out as a sweet idea of Mr. Hooper's: have the eight of us employees at Pepparooni's choose names from a Santa mug, then spend a maximum of nine dollars on the recipient. Easy.

For most of us, slinging slices at Pepparooni's is our first job, so everyone got pretty into it. Mona literally CROCHETED something for Addie. Naomi made it super clear that she had a crush on Logan with the hot-glued picture frame (side note: when did hearts start denoting Christmas?). I pulled Georgia (got her a seven-dollar plant that she didn't even pretend to like, but that's another story). Liam pulled me.

Let's talk about Liam. He's sixteen, founder of the Film Appreci-ation club, in AP Physics already (which is amazing), and very, very, so obviously has a crush on me (and has, BTW, since we were in sixth grade). And here's the thing. I like him. I just don't like like him. He's friend material, a hundred percent.

Anyway, none of that really matters until later.

On the twenty-third, the last day Hooper scheduled any of us at the pizzeria for three days, we had this mini holiday party. Elf hats (required), free pizza (I'm still not sick of it), soda, and ice cream bars. Like I said, Mr. Hooper is really sweet.

So Liam pulled my name—Adriana. And, since he knows me, he knows I love *Stardew Valley*. I'm basically playing it on my phone during every break, and I even tried to get a club started at school until I couldn't find a teacher-advisor. Adults, I'd found, often don't pay attention to what kids are interested in until it matters to them.

The package with my name on it wasn't wrapped that well, but it was small and covered in tape, so it took me forever to unwrap it. When I did, it was literally this tiny, little computer chip with a mini version of a Junimo—my favorite creature from *Stardew Valley*, pixelated and everything—in this deep, metallic green. It was weird and I loved it.

"OMG, who got this for me?" I sputtered and looked around.

But I didn't have to do much investigating. Liam was literally turning bright red and wouldn't look at me. So I punched him in the shoulder.

"You got this for me? *How* was this less than nine dollars?"

Now everyone was looking and asking to see, so Liam had no choice but to explain. "It was just in my dad's junk drawer in his office. I tweaked it a little . . ."

I nudged him. "Look at you, all artsy."

He laughed, and his cheeks returned to their normal color.

We spent the rest of the party huddled and chatting, and, maybe it was the unlimited Mountain Dew talking or the ice cream bar or the twinkling Christmas lights or the snow falling outside the window, but I actually LIKED talking to him. Like, a lot.

As person after person left, elf hat crammed on their heads, the party was clearing up and he asked, "You want a ride home?"

I nodded, then texted my parents that they didn't need to come get me, which prompted a flurry of questions. But, like I said, I've known Liam forever, so my parents trusted him.

Sending those texts? That was the last mundane thing I did.

I don't know if it was because he was nervous—he seemed it!—or what, but Liam didn't suggest leaving until it was just us and Mr. Hooper, who was cleaning everything up the way my mom does when she wants dinner guests to leave.

"Should we go?" I asked.

Liam nodded like he was thinking the same thing. "Thanks, Mr. Hooper. And Happy Holidays!"

"Happy Holidays, kids. Now get home safe." He waved and moved toward the lights to shut down the whole operation.

"Get home safe." Those words would echo in my mind more times than he could ever have imagined.

We stepped out into the quiet, that kind of muffled vibe of tons of snow falling and coating everything. I think we both felt it, because we were quiet the whole way to Liam's truck, an old red pickup that his dad had given him when he got his license.

"Sorry, it's kind of messy." He tried to clean up fast, but I didn't mind.

"No problem." I relocated a water bottle and sweatshirt and got in.

We drove for a while, and that same feeling of slight nervousness— why? It's just Liam!—came back to me. But the longer we didn't say anything, the weirder it got.

When we finally spoke, it was at the same time.

"So what are you—" We both stopped, then giggled.

"Go ahead," Liam said.

I shook my head. "Oh, nothing. I was just going to ask what you're doing for Christmas."

"My grandparents are coming in from Chicago. Tomorrow morning. You?" He glanced at me, then back at the snowy road.

"Grandparents coming in from Boston."

I laughed at the similarity of our plans. Then the conversation fizzled into more nerves. I beat myself up a little because I definitely didn't like him, but all of a sudden I couldn't think straight much less talk.

Wondering if Liam was feeling the same, even just a little bit, I let my eyes wander to his face. But he had a strange look on his face as he glanced in the rearview mirror at the bright headlights of the car behind us. He looked worried.

"What's wrong?" I asked, turning to squint into blinding headlights.

"Nothing. Just . . . it just seems like that car is following us. It's made the same turn as us twice."

I shielded my eyes from the headlights but couldn't make out anything. Glancing at Liam, I could see he looked stressed—he's a little high-strung—so I thought I'd go for an eensy-weensy bit of fun.

"Let's try to lose him!" I dared, voice edging on shrill.

And if there's something to know about Liam, it's that he's a literalist. All of a sudden, he hung a sharp left, so I was kind of smushed against the window and had to hang on tight.

"Sorry," he muttered, but without his usual attention. His eyes were still on the car behind us, which took the turn as fast as we did and seemed to be getting closer.

"Hang on." Liam, like some racecar driver, like some daredevil, like someone I don't know, yanked the steering wheel in the other direction, screeching into a U-turn. I ended up toppling toward him, losing my grip on the mini Junimo.

"My present!" As the words left my mouth, I realized how dumb they were, considering our possible situation.

Liam didn't respond, just punched the gas and we blew past the last exit to Crystal Lake, the last road that would take us home.

When I spoke, it was in a low whisper. "Where are we going?"

"I don't know. Somewhere this car won't follow us."

I spotted the exit for Christmas Tree Lane and pointed. "Maybe?"

I knew it'd be packed, even with the snow. Liam gave a quick nod and waited, then swerved to the exit just before we passed it, sending me banging into his shoulder again.

"Sorry!" We both shouted as the wheels screeched and snow flew.

We bounced off the exit with Liam pumping the brakes. The truck skidded to a stop just touching a snow bank. We looked at each other.

"Did we lose them?" I breathed.

Liam nodded without blinking. "I think so?"

Crowds passed beside us, talking and laughing. The normalcy of the whole place put an exclamation point on my jittery nerves.

Liam felt around the floor, then handed me my Junimo.

"Thanks." I tucked it into my belt bag, where I should have kept it all along. My hands shook as I struggled with the zipper.

Liam noticed. "Want to get lost in the crowd? Shake off the weird-ness?"

"Yeah. And I seriously need to go to the bathroom."

We clambered out of the pickup, walked half a block, and then I excused myself while Liam looked for hot chocolate.

When I came back out, Liam was wearing his elf hat from the

Christmas party. He put mine on my head. "Disguise in case we need it."

I rolled my eyes and laughed. My heartbeat slowed for the first time since I'd seen the headlights behind us.

Pointy, green felt hats on, we made our way through booths selling peppermint-scented candles, handmade wreaths with live holly berries, and stockings with little frames for pet photos.

We started chatting about all the holly and candy canes around us, letting our creepy arrival fade into the past.

"The best presents are the ones you didn't even ask for," Liam argued and, while I'd usually find a reason to debate, after tonight's gift exchange, I had to agree.

"How *did* you know I liked Junimos? I don't think we've ever even talked about it, have we?"

Maybe it was the cold, but I could have sworn Liam blushed again. So I punched him in the shoulder—again. "Are you spying on me?"

"What? No! I . . . you've mentioned it before, that's all." He lifted his eyes to mine and now it was my turn to blush. When did his eyes get so blue?

I moved my gaze to the ground so I could concentrate. "Well, I do talk about it a lot. It's fun! I mean, you've played, right?"

The silence said a lot. I stopped cold. "You've never played?"

He squinted like he was trying to decide whether to lie, then shook his head.

I whipped out my phone and pulled up *Stardew Valley*. A gust of wind fluttered both of our elf hats, and I stepped back into the doorway of the City Hall building—three stories of brick that announced to the world that this is the most important building in town.

Liam looked over my shoulder, and I could feel the tip of his elf hat brush my hair. But I persevered, pretending not to be distracted.

"See, you just choose where you want to—" I glanced up, and that's when I saw it: the car that had been chasing us. It was idling, lights off, across the street. Like whoever was in there was watching us.

Liam saw it, too. I could see his breath come out in a slow exhale. "Is that them?"

Liam nodded, almost imperceptibly. Then, in a whisper, "Follow me."

We turned, yanked the door to the building and raced inside. The laughter and music from the street became muffled. We looked at each other.

"Now what?" I asked.

"We call our parents."

We grabbed our phones, but before we could do anything, the door behind us swung open. Liam grabbed my hand, and we raced to the stairs.

Taking the steps two at a time, we only stopped running when there were no more stairs. We'd reached the top of the building. As I panted, I could make out the sound of footsteps. I looked, scared, at Liam.

"Come on!" He threw open the doors to a small balcony that I'm sure was more decorative than anything else.

"But there's nowhere left to go!" I leaned over the balcony and tried to guess our chances. Maybe if we aimed for a snowdrift, we wouldn't break every bone in our bodies?

We both leaned over and watched as Liam's elf hat fluttered away. Then we heard a creak behind us.

We turned slowly and saw the door opening. Without thinking, I jumped onto the railing, then slipped. As I spun around, my belt bag hooked onto a metal spire on the railing, keeping me afloat, three stories above the Christmas crowd that was happily, and cluelessly, going about their evening.

I dangled there, like an elfin piñata, blinking at the hard, icy pavement below. The sounds of the holiday crowd disappeared. For a silent moment, I watched my breath come out in cold puffs as the world continued merrily beneath me. I blinked in wonder at just how wrong a pizza party could go.

Sound slowly returned, the pounding of my heart filled my ears.

Then, through the shock: "Liam!"

It was a man's voice, punctuated by heavy footsteps.

"Dad! What are you—Help me!" Liam's voice was shrill, panicked.

And just like that, two sets of hands pulled me back onto the balcony.

"Liam, why were you running?" The gruff voice belonged to a man with a trim gray beard, broad shoulders, and the same blue eyes as Liam. I may have made a mental note of the exact shade of blue earlier in the night.

Liam threw up his hands. "Dad! Was that you? Chasing us?"

"No!" He sputtered, stumbling over himself. "My agents were tracking you. Of course they didn't recognize your truck. Why would they? It was only when I got here—after they called—that I saw it was you. I'm just glad I got to you before they did!" He shuddered.

"Dad." Liam shook his head.

"Let's go inside." The man—I mean, Liam's DAD??—led us in off the balcony.

My head was spinning. I was freezing, scared, and confused. Liam's dad walked us all the way down to the street, then sat us in a warm café, bought us hot chocolate, and pulled up a stool to explain.

He rubbed his beard like he was uncomfortable, then stuck out his hand to me, half manners, half apology. "Gerald. I'm Liam's dad."

I glanced at Liam, who had that rosy glow to his cheeks again. Then I shook Gerald's hand. "I'm Adriana."

"You're—" He looked at Liam, whose blush flamed a brighter red, if that was possible.

Gerald shook his head. "I'm so, so sorry for this mix-up. You see, that chip. It's sort of important."

"Wait . . . is that why the car was chasing us?" I fumbled for my little Junimo, then held it up in the light.

"Well, not the . . . whatever Liam turned it into. But the chip, yes. It has a tracker on it."

Liam shifted impatiently. "If it's important government property, why was it in the junk drawer?"

"The agency needed me to test how far away I could track it, and hiding it at home just made sense. And you know the junk drawer is the only place in the house that doesn't get organized. No one bothers with it."

Liam shook his head, and I felt bad for him. He'd actually paid attention to what I liked. He'd seen something that reminded him of it, and he decided to make something for me. That's, like 5 out of 5. And now, he's sitting here like he's in trouble.

I nudged him, but this time, it was soft and friendly. And it got a smile out of him. "Hey, it's okay."

"I'm really sorry," Liam said, his voice and shoulders low.

"Why? I thought the best part of the night would be the pizza. But you took me on an adventure." I smiled at him, and this time didn't look away when his blue eyes met mine. Something about what we'd been through that night made it feel like we were snowed in together, in a secret, secluded place where no one else knew how funny and kind and brave we'd been together.

Gerald drove us home. He said we'd been through too much that night for more driving. But he was nice enough to stay in the car when Liam offered to walk me to my door.

"Thanks for the ride." I waved to Gerald. He shook his head.

"It's the least I could do."

At my front door, Liam shook his head and we both laughed a little, feeling the nerves come back. "I'm honestly not sure what to say."

"It's been a weird night."

He nodded, and I felt like there was only one thing to do. I took his hand. He raised his eyes to mine.

"Thank you for the present."

"Sorry you had to give it back."

I shrugged then stepped toward him and kissed him on the cheek, and I swear I could feel him starting to blush at the touch. "Merry Christmas," I whispered.

He smiled. "Merry Christmas."

I hurried in before either of us could say anything else, before we could second-guess anything, and before anything could pop that perfect bubble of a night—an adventure—together.

About the Author

Justine Gunn writes rom-coms full of heart, humor, and humanity for film, TV, and print. She has been included in the holiday romance anthologies *The Gift Exchange* and *12 Knights of Christmas*, and has written for the Hallmark Channel's *Cooking with Love* and Lifetime's *Holly's Holiday.* A former fencer and expat and current Packer owner, parent, and cancer survivor, she writes characters who overcome obstacles with laughter and love. She has cowritten a Valentine's-themed feature for Jim Henson Productions and written on the Emmy-nominated preschool show *Tab Time.*

You can follow Justine on Instagram at:
@justinegunnwrites

Tater
Tot

Tater Tot

Desi Stowe

Chapter 1

The scratches on my skin hurt my pride more than my arm, but the raw claw marks still sting. It hurts worse when Veronica, my boss, insists she clean the injury with hydrogen peroxide.

What is even the point of hydrogen peroxide? It must be some kind of medieval punishment that has lived on through time. Adults like to say it kills the germs. I say it's an excuse to torture kids when they're already suffering. Besides, adults are obsessed with cleanliness and killing off germs these days. *It's annoying.*

Veronica smiles at me. She's a happy person, which makes me wonder if she's even a full-fledged adult.

Adults are not happy people.

They beg you to enjoy your childhood and to eat, like, broccoli. I get I need to eat vegetables, but please don't give me broccoli. *Gross.*

You can't be happy and eat broccoli at the same time. That's probably why they're unhappy. They've eaten too much broccoli.

Veronica smooths the bandage on my hand. "She got you good this time." She's a great boss. She owns the cat shelter close to my house. *Best. Job. Ever.*

Inspecting the bandage, I let out a sigh. The kind my dad would say is filled with "teenage angst."

"Yeah, she got me good." *She* is Tater Tot, an orange tabby cat who's a bit temperamental.

"Did you exercise patience?" Veronica looks amused. She already knows the answer.

I laugh and shake my head. "Eh, probably not."

Patience is another thing adults are always pushing on us. It's not like they have any of it, though. If I'd been patient with Tater Tot, I probably wouldn't be sporting a new set of angry red stripes. Maybe I should get a tattoo of cat claw marks when I'm older. Trevor, my big brother, said he'd take me when I turn eighteen. My parents hate tattoos. My brother loves making them squirm.

Veronica gives me a long, understanding look. I appreciate that she's not taking this incident as a teaching moment or a chance to lecture me. I get lectured enough.

I finish my work sweeping scattered litter and refilling water dishes. I'm too young for a real job, a paying job. I'm only fourteen. But I volunteer at the cat shelter. That's how much I love cats.

The bell on the door jingles, and I see my dad walk in wearing a Christmas sweater with a moose that has lights tangled in its antlers. My dad is . . . a festive one. Never met an ugly Christmas sweater *he* didn't like. He rocks the holiday wear for at least a month. We make fun of him, of course. But I think that only encourages him more.

"Hey, Dad. Let me say bye to Tater Tot."

Dad chuckles. He's used to me stalling. He jokes that I'd sleep here if they let me. "Sure thing, JoAnna Banana."

I hate being called JoAnna Banana. It's been Dad's nickname for me since forever, though. The nickname was cute when I was little, but I'm a teenager now, with an image to maintain.

My image? I'm the nerdy girl with hair that's too curly and cat fur on my clothes, even though I carry a lint roller everywhere. I don't care, though. Did I mention I love cats? But my parents won't let me adopt one. Dad says he "doesn't need more stress." Mom doesn't say much about it. I secretly think she wants a cat, too.

My fingertips reach into Tater Tot's cage. She sniffs my fingers in an apology for scratching me earlier. She's a tiny little thing, but the way she eats makes me think she'll be a full-sized cat soon.

"More scratches?" Dad asks. He looks a little worried, but then again, he's always worried.

My hands are small enough to reach in the enclosure and scratch Tater Tot behind the ears, right where she likes it. If that's all I'd done earlier, I wouldn't have new scratches. But I'd tried to pick her up. She wasn't ready for that.

Dad rubs his hand over the back of my head, and it says everything he's already said to me. "Now's not a good time for a pet, JoAnna Banana."

Leaving Tater Tot behind hurts me on the inside, like actual physical pain. I'd even be happy if someone else adopted her. She needs a home; it doesn't have to be mine. But there's no sense in arguing with Dad about it. Again.

"Goodnight, Veronica!"

She beams. "Goodnight to my best employee!"

"Still feels like you should be paying me!"

Dad shakes his head, but Veronica only laughs. I ask her to pay me every time I'm here. It'd be weird if I stopped.

Dad and I walk out together. "Your mom is home, making breakfast for dinner."

"Yay!" I *love* breakfast for dinner; it's my favorite. I need a bright spot in my day. Plus, this means Mom has forgiven me for my outburst yesterday. *Excessive* teenage angst, Dad called it.

Dad starts with the inevitable parent questions. "How was school?"

"Ugh." School today was hard. I'm convinced my science teacher is an alien. No one from this planet should be *that* excited about photosynthesis. Then we had a surprise quiz in math. There was a fight in the lunchroom next to my table, and my tray of food got knocked to the floor. The teacher wouldn't let me get a replacement tray and acted like the mess was my fault.

Right. Those two girls have been fighting since second grade.

Dad gives me a crooked smile and then backs out of the parking space. "Ah, the teenage angst, I see."

My eyes focus on the world outside my window. Festive decorations and lights. Everything looks so happy. I wish I could be happy. Instead, I only feel stressed today.

"Tell me about this orange cat."

I turn my head away from the window. Is he dropping the topic of school? That's suspicious. "Really?"

We're stopped at the traffic light, so Dad turns to look at me. "If this orange cat is important to you, then I want to know about it. Besides, she's cute. Shy, but a mischievous glint in her eyes. Bet she's smart, too. Reminds me of my daughter."

My dad is one hundred percent a total dork. But he does love me, and I'm old enough to know that not everyone has a dad like that.

"Her name is Tater Tot. All the kittens in her litter were named after some kind of fast food. Cheeseburger and French Fry were adopted together last week."

"That's adorable." He chuckles.

Most of my brain wants to shut down the conversation and sulk about my bad day. But cats are fun to talk about. "You have to take your time getting to know her; that's why no one has adopted her."

"She's skittish?"

"Yeah, that's a good word for her. If I move too fast, she'll scratch me." I hold up my arm. "But she's not mean. She's just scared."

"I see. Animals act out when they're scared. People, too."

And there it is. Dad is about to turn this into a life lesson. I don't hate it, but I don't love it, either. I wasn't the best daughter yesterday. Time to roll with it instead of fighting it like I usually do.

"Do you mean like when I threw the glass across the room? After you guys told me Trevor isn't coming home for the holidays?"

My big brother left for college this year. In Chicago, of all places. The land of endless snow. All flights going out of Chicago were grounded due to a huge snowstorm going through the city. I miss him so, so much. I broke a glass out of anger when Mom told me he won't be here.

"Does Trevor's not being here scare you?"

I look out the window again because I don't want Dad to see the tears trying to form. "He's got this big, fancy college life now. He's probably forgotten all about me." My words sound more grumpy than fearful. But I am scared I've lost my brother. Earlier, I texted him a super-cute picture of Tater Tot. He didn't even answer.

"Trevor hasn't forgotten you. He just got snowed in. All of the flights were canceled." He takes a deep breath. "Your Mom and I are sad about it, too."

"He's so far away." My voice breaks a bit. My emotions are too much today. They feel like they are too much too often these days. Mom says it's part of growing up.

Dad squeezes my shoulder. "He'd be here if he could."

My shoulders feel tense. "Are we just gonna have Christmas without him?"

Since we were little, Trevor and I would sleep in our loft and watch Christmas movies late into the night Christmas Eve. Even when he got a driver's license and was hardly ever home, we'd still always have our holiday movie marathon together. I don't think I can do it without him.

Dad rubs his hand over his beard. He turns the car onto our street. "We can video call him in."

Hastily, I wipe my eyes. "That's not the same."

Before we go inside, Dad pulls me into a hug. "I wish I could fix it, JoAnna Banana."

"I wish you could, too."

Chapter 2

Today is the last day before the holiday break, which is the only good thing about today. Before I walk into school, I check my phone. Trevor finally texted me back late last night: *Please tell me you talked the parents into adopting her.*

I grin and send back: *if only*

I stash my phone as my best friend, Zoe, catches up to me.

"Hey, Jo! Ready for science?"

Groaning, I roll my eyes. Zoe loves science. Wants to be a paleontologist. She somehow has been able to ignore the fact that our teacher is clearly an extraterrestrial being.

She bumps shoulders with me. "Hey, it's the last day before the holiday break. What's wrong?"

It's a subject I don't want to talk about, but Zoe won't let it go until I tell her. That's a great quality in a best friend. It's also an awful one. "Trevor's flight got canceled because of snow. He's not coming home."

Her eyes are sympathetic. She gets me. "Lame! He can't get another flight?"

"I guess not." I change the subject to something that's still just the worst but hurts a little less. "Plus, Tater Tot probably isn't going to be adopted before Christmas."

"The orange kitty? Your parents are still saying no?"

"Ugh." I roll my eyes again.

"It could be worse, ya know. I want a Micropachycephalosaurus. But. . ." She heaves a deep sigh and shakes her head. "Those are extinct."

"Okay. . ."

A voice as familiar as it is annoying fills the air behind me. "Out of my way, Slow Mo Jo." Zach shoves me into my locker, and a pain shoots up my left arm. Then he turns back and winks at me, like getting shoved around is all fun and games.

Zoe grabs my elbow, and we weave our way through the other students so we can make it to class on time. "I *hate* that guy. You alright?"

Zach has annoyed me all year. He's in most of my classes, of course. "I'm fine." Talking about Zach is also the worst, so I change the subject. "What's your second choice for an extinct animal pet? After micropach—"

"A Micropachycephalosaurus? Probably an Archaeopteryx. They can fly, though. So I'm not sure how that would work." She slides into her seat.

"Jo, why are you hanging out with Dino Dork when you can hang out with us?" Zach's obnoxiousness makes another unwelcome appearance. Trevor told me that Zach probably likes me. As in, *likes me*, likes me. He said some guys are mean to you when they like you. He also said those kinds of guys are stupid and a waste of my time. As if I'd ever be interested in Zach, of all people. I already knew some guys acted like that; I've known that since third grade. But we're in high school now, and I thought things might be different. Trevor laughed when I said that, so I guess not.

"Go away, Zach," I mutter.

Zach starts doing this awful dance backward. The worst attempt at a moon walk, ever. He's so arrogant, he doesn't even know it's terrible.

The Gift Exchange

That's when it happens. Zach trips over a backpack strap and falls back, landing on his butt with a thud. His cheeks pinken as everyone laughs. I'd feel bad for anyone else. But this guy had it coming. I stifle a laugh and take my seat.

Our science teacher from outer space yells out, "Quiet, everyone!!"

He walks to the front of the room, propping up on the desk. "We've only got one more science class before your brains rot from candy and excessive screen time while you're on holiday break. When you get back, we're going to dissect cow eyeballs!"

"Cool," Zoe whispers from the desk behind me.

"Gross," I say at the exact same time.

The rest of the day consists of teachers who are just as excited for the break as we are. In art class, Ms. Shale lets us free sketch. With a burnt-orange color pencil, I draw Tater Tot, using muted yellow to shade in around the face and paws. My blending has improved this year, and I've learned a lot in art class.

Ms. Shale inspects my drawing. "Nice work, Jo." She beams at me. I tell her all about working at the shelter and Tater Tot. Ms. Shale started teaching art this year; it's her first real job. She's barely an adult; she's not grumpy like the others. She gives me some tips about outlining around the eyes and claws to help the drawing "pop."

Sketching helps me feel less stressed; it's soothing. Ms. Shale has helped improve my sketching and taught me to add color to it. My mom said how much my drawings have improved, and she hung one on the refrigerator like I was still five years old. It's only kind of annoying. As I pack up my things at the end of class, I wonder if my parents would like a sketch as a gift for Christmas. Maybe I can draw my dad in one of his silly sweaters.

Ms. Shale hugs me as I linger after class. Next is math, and I'd rather stay in art class. The hug feels nice and warm.

I'd like to give Ms. Shale a holiday gift; she's always so nice to me. But it seems weird, and I feel too awkward to do it. I feel bad that I don't have anything for her; she's the best teacher.

"Excited for the holidays?" she asks.

Am I? I'm so sad about my brother not coming home and Tater Tot not being adopted. But I love the idea of a break from school, and Mom said we could bake cookies together. "It's complicated," I say, finally settling on an answer.

She chuckles. "Life is often complicated."

Chapter 3

The next day, my plan was to sleep in and then spend the whole afternoon helping Veronica get everything ready so she can leave the cats at the shelter for a few days while she goes and visits her mom. I told her I could check on the cats for her while she's gone, but I think she's hesitant to give me the keys because I'm a kid. She has a friend coming to check on the cats. *A grown-up.*

Mom said I could ride my bike to the shelter as long as I came home before dark. The cold air bites my skin as I ride the two miles of trail between my house and the shelter. The exercise and the freedom from school melt some of my stress away. Maybe today will be the day Tater Tot lets me hold her. Or maybe she'll even climb into my lap. If I work on my responsibilities quickly, I might have enough time to be patient with her.

My happiness fades as I see Veronica sitting on the steps to the shelter with her head buried in her hands.

"Veronica?" I lay my bike against the side of the building and take off my helmet.

"Jo, sweet girl. I've got some bad news." She wipes her eyes, and I brace for the worst. "Tater Tot got out when I had a big delivery come in. She slid right out of her cage and disappeared out the back door. I can't find her."

My heart plummets to the ground and lands in a pile of sorrow and anxiety. "When?"

"This morning, just before lunch."

"I can help look for her." My teeth clench as determination fills me up on the inside. Tater Tot will not stay lost. Not if I can help it.

"I put up signs around the neighborhood behind us." She shakes her head. "The worst part is that I had someone stop by and adopt her this morning. But she wanted to leave Tater Tot at the shelter while she picked up food and a carrier."

"We've *got* to find her." Never have I wanted something more than I want to find this kitten.

"The lady who came by, you know her, Amelia Shale. Said you drew a picture of Tater Tot, and she fell in love with her when she saw the picture. Came by, and that skittish kitten let her scratch behind her ears. Didn't even run away."

"Ms. Shale. My art teacher. Everyone loves her." My heart hurts. What if we can't find Tater Tot? She's the perfect pet for Ms. Shale. They're perfect for each other. Finding Tater Tot would be the best gift for her. And for Tater Tot.

"Tater Tot might be back for dinner. I had another cat escape a couple of years ago. After two days of being gone, he came back at dinner time." She pauses to rub my back. "That little kitten is a smart one. I'm trying not to worry too much about it." She sighs. "Why don't you come inside? I want you to meet our new cat. Her name is Wilma. She's about ten years old."

I hesitate to follow her, glancing up and down the street and hoping to catch a blur of orange fur, but eventually do go inside to meet Wilma.

The older cats don't always get adopted. People prefer kittens. Wilma is sweet and purrs against my leg. But I can't focus. I'm so worried about Tater Tot.

Veronica and I get Wilma's enclosure set up quickly. Wilma must like it because she's already curled up on her bed and napping. Then we spent the next couple of hours looking for Tater Tot without any luck. I text my parents that I need a ride home since it's kind of late.

Veronica looks at me, and her eyes are sad. "I've got to go. My flight leaves soon."

I'm mad that Veronica is leaving when we haven't found Tater Tot. But I also get that she needs to see her mom, and plane tickets are expensive. Her mom probably wants to see her as much as I want to see Trevor. "I'll keep looking for Tater Tot."

"I probably shouldn't give you a key to the shelter, but I want you to have it in case you find her, so you can put her back in her enclosure."

"I can do this, I'm responsible. I won't lose the key."

"I know you are, but it's not fair of me to give you an adult responsibility." She looks conflicted. "Especially on your holiday break. Tater Tot escaped from the top of the enclosure. I already fixed the area she squeezed out of."

A familiar voice speaks next to me, startling me, because I didn't hear anyone else come in. "I'll help her. Whatever she needs, she doesn't have to do it alone."

"Trevor?!" This time the tears flood my eyes, and I can't keep them from spilling over. My big brother is here.

"He's my brother," I explain to Veronica while hugging him.

My brother puts his hands on my shoulders and looks at me. "What's going on?"

"Tater Tot is missing!" I'm still crying. I'm so happy and so sad. It's complicated.

"The cat from your text message?"

"Yeah," I sniffle.

He squeezes my upper arms. "Okay. Then we have to find her."

Veronica has to leave, but I'm not alone. I've got my big brother to help me now. He actually made it home! And he wants to help. Together, I'm sure we can find Tater Tot. *Everything is going to be okay.*

Chapter 4

Breakfast the next morning is full of yummy food. My mom cooks when she's happy. She's ecstatic that Trevor made it home. He ended up taking two flights to get here, but he made it. He and I looked for Tater Tot yesterday until it was too dark to even see. No sign of the kitten.

This morning, we all laughed and celebrated being together over the delicious food. But there's still a gnawing anxiety in the pit of my stomach. Veronica says cats are very smart and don't really need us. What if Tater Tot needs us, though? She's only a baby. Plus, Ms. Shale needs her.

Trevor asks if Zach is still causing me trouble, and I tell him he pushed me into a locker. Our parents get mad because they didn't know about it. But I didn't think it was that big of a deal.

"It doesn't matter anyway. He tripped and fell in science class, and everyone laughed at him." I eat more scrambled eggs and grab another muffin. I'm starving this morning. I've been so worried about Tater Tot that I've barely eaten. I'm still worried, but I need food if I'm going to look for her. I hope Mom is cool with me looking for her again. I know she had family plans for us.

On cue, Mom asks, "What should we do today?"

Trevor gets another plate of food. "I'm looking for Tater Tot."

I look at my parents nervously before my eyes meet Trevor's. "You are?"

Dad tilts his chin. He's wearing a snowman sweater. This one has bells sewn into it, so it jingles. "That settles it. We're all looking for Tater Tot."

Mom agrees. My family is so annoying sometimes, but they're also the absolute *best*. It's not super cold outside, but Mom still insists we all bundle up. Zoe sends me a text, and she's coming to help look for Tater Tot, too. We've got lots of people looking, so I'm sure we'll find her. *We've got to.*

We look all day. We stop for lunch, and Dad buys everyone food from the taco truck down the street. Zoe, too. But then she has to go home.

"Let me know the second you find her." She gives me a big hug, and I feel some of my sadness melt away.

A few minutes after Zoe leaves, Ms. Shale runs up to me. "I've been looking for Tater Tot all day."

"Us, too! Veronica said you adopted her. We're going to find her because she'll have the best home with you." I throw my arms around her. I know you're not supposed to love teachers. But I love Ms. Shale.

She gives me her number. "If you find her, call me and I'll come take her home right away! I'm going to come back and look some more later today."

Trevor and I look in the woods behind the shelter while our parents look in the neighborhood. My mom loves talking, so she's been telling everyone about our missing kitten and giving out her phone number. I much prefer the quiet of the woods.

Trevor glances at me and grins. "So, how old do you think Ms. Shale might be? Twenty-three? Twenty-four?"

I laugh. "She's too old for you. And too pretty."

He grabs his chest. "Ouch, you hurt me."

Naturally, I continue. "And way too smart."

"Ah, it's alright. I might have a girlfriend. Don't tell Mom, though; she'd get way too excited." He cringes.

"She totally would. What do you mean she 'might' be your girl-friend? Please tell me you're not being mean to her just to get her attention."

I drop to my knees and look under a fallen log that has a hole the size of a small animal. I pull out my phone and use the flashlight feature to look inside. No luck.

"I mean, we've been hanging out. I like her." He smiles. "I think you'd like her, too."

I'm not sure anyone is good enough for my big brother. But he seems happy, and that makes me happy. "I probably would."

"Need me to threaten this Zach guy while I'm in town?" He calls out for Tater Tot and looks under a pile of sticks.

"Ugh, no. He's not worth your time. Or mine."

"Atta girl." He tousles my hair. "Anyone around that might be worth your time?"

I blush. "There's a guy in my art class that I kind of like. He's quiet. But I just found out he doesn't like cats. He likes reptiles. He has a pet snake. *On purpose.* As in he wanted to befriend a snake and made him part of his family. He drew an awesome picture of the snake and showed it to me." I shudder at the thought of someone actually wanting to keep a snake in their house. I always run away from them.

This makes Trevor laugh. "That would be a hard gap to bridge."

"You're telling me."

We talk and laugh. But still no sign of Tater Tot. It's getting late, so we head home, and my chest squeezes in fear that we might not be able to find her. Mom helps me frame my drawing of Tater Tot, and I wrap it in snowflake paper for Ms. Shale. It's not as good as finding Tater Tot, but I want to give her something so she knows she's a great teacher.

Mom smiles at me, "I think it's a great gift."

Chapter 5

It's pretty late, but I'm sitting on the porch and worrying about the sweet, shy kitten who's lost and maybe even scared. The thick blanket I have tucked around me keeps me warm. We haven't had any snow yet, but it's getting cold. I can't help but think that Tater Tot needs us; she needs Ms. Shale. But none of that matters. Not if we can't find her.

Mom called all the veterinarian clinics and let them know that Tater Tot was missing, just in case someone dropped her off at a clinic. I didn't even think to do that. I hugged her and told her I was sorry we hadn't had time to make cookies together. She said we can make cookies to celebrate finding Tater Tot instead. She wasn't even mad about it.

Dad comes out to join me on the porch, wearing reindeer onesie pajamas. He's given up some of the holiday festivities, too, to help me find Tater Tot. And clearly, Dad loves festivities. The past couple of days have been full of worry. But I've also realized that maybe I'm not as alone as I've been feeling lately. Maybe the best gift ever is having a family that cares about you.

Dad doesn't say anything at first. Just sits with his arm around me and sways back and forth with me on our porch swing. I break the silence. "Do you think I've wasted everyone's time today?"

He hugs me closer, and I lay my head on his shoulder. "I think that whatever is important to you is important to the people who love you. That's never time wasted."

"Like it's important for you to wear ridiculous holiday gear? And it's important that I let you do it without making fun of you?"

He laughs. "But you do make fun of me."

"Not as much as I want to."

He's quiet for a minute, watching the night sky. "The stars are bright tonight. You see a lot of star decorations this time of year."

"Like the one on our tree?"

"Yeah. The star symbolizes different things to different people."

I know the story of the shepherds being guided by a bright star. But I never thought about it symbolizing more than that. I don't say anything. But the thought swirls in my brain.

Dad continues, "Some people see a star as a guiding light. Literally and figuratively. Some say it symbolizes that we're never alone, someone out there is watching over us."

I snuggle into my dad's side further,

"Do you want to know what the star means to me?"

I look up at him.

"To me, a star means that the light of hope exists, even in our darkest times."

"Even times when we can't find a sweet but stubborn kitten?"

"Even then. Or even when kids are mean to you at school. Or when you have a test. Hope is even there when your entire life feels like it's unraveling at the seams." He smooths out my hair, which I'm sure is a tangled mess. "Hope is the greatest of gifts."

We sit there in silence as I think about hope. About it being a *gift*. Hope feels big, like I can't even wrap my arms around it enough to pull it to me, so I feel it on the inside. But Dad said hope is there. And maybe I make fun of him for his reindeer pajamas. And maybe I think he's a dork. But he's also right about a lot of things. I think he might be right about hope, too.

I close my eyes and think of Tater Tot. About how she likes to climb to the top of her enclosure and look out the window. She likes to watch the birds in the tree right outside the window.

That's when it hits me. We've been doing our search wrong. Tater Tot is skittish. I bet she didn't go far from the shelter. And she hates holes and small places. She likes being up high.

"Dad! I think I know where Tater Tot might be."

He looks at me and smiles. He doesn't look worried or tired. He looks excited. "Okay. Let's go get her."

Chapter 6

Mom and Trevor come, too, because this whole debacle has turned into a family affair. Not gonna lie, I love it. I love that they're here for me and for Tater Tot. And I love that my brother is here. He said he didn't want to tell me he was still trying to get home; he worried he might get delayed elsewhere. But all the time, he kept trying to get home to see us.

"What made you think you needed to look in the tree by the shelter?" Mom asks. I'd just told everyone about how Tater Tot liked to be high. She liked watching the birds in that particular tree.

"While Dad and I were outside, he told me about finding hope and stars. It made me think that I should look up. Literally."

Mom squeezes Dad's shoulder. "We fell in love under a starry night sky."

Trevor looks at me. "I've got twenty bucks for you if you have ear-buds to give me to drown out all of this," he looks at our parents and gestures wildly, "romantic talk."

Everyone laughs except Trevor. No earbuds needed, since Dad is pulling into the shelter's parking lot. The car has barely rolled to a stop before I'm scrambling out of my seat and toward the tree next to the shelter.

Looking up, I can't see anything—no cat in sight. Surely, I can't be wrong. All this talk about stars and hope has to mean something.

"Tater Tot?"

Dad pushes a flashlight into my hand.

My ears strain, and I hear the faintest meow. My eyes keep searching as I circle to the other side of the tree. In the crook of a branch, barely visible, is a tiny orange kitten.

"Tater Tot! She's here!" And my family starts cheering. I motion frantically for them to keep quiet. I don't want to scare her away. "I don't think she can get down."

Dad takes the keys to the shelter to see if he can find anything to help. I text Ms. Shale and Veronica that we've found Tater Tot and we're trying to get her down. My mind scurries in fifteen different directions, trying to problem-solve.

"Mom, you're not going to like this," I say as I settle on a solution.

"You're going to have to climb up to get her, aren't you?" She looks worried but resolved. She trusts me to do this task, to rescue this sweet kitten. But she's a mom, so she has to worry. It's part of the job description.

Trevor holds out his hands. "Let me give you a boost."

I step on his intertwined fingers and grab onto the lowest branch. Tree climbing is fun. I used to do it all the time. But this tree doesn't have many lower branches. Not sure how I'll get down, not sure how I'll convince Tater Tot to let me hold her, not sure if any of this is going to work, but I'm gonna try. I've *got* to, so that when Ms. Shale comes, I can give her Tater Tot *and* my gift. My backpack is still in the car, with the gift inside. When I thought I figured out where Tater Tot was, I put it in the car just in case the night turned out the way I was hoping it would. I've just got to get Tater Tot out of his tree safely.

I've got people here who love and support me. With their help, I can figure this out.

My arms struggle with the challenge, and my hands hurt as the bark of the tree digs into them. It's hard, but I pull myself up, and

I think that maybe when I trained for the pull-up bar test in P.E., I should've put more effort into it. The next branch is closer, and I can reach it easily. I sit on that branch. Tater Tot is within reach. She mews at me.

"I'm going to have to sit here a little bit. Veronica says Tater Tot needs patience."

Dad comes out with a portable carrier and a step ladder he found in the storage closet. He sets it up near the base of the tree while I talk to the scared kitten in calm, soothing tones.

"You're going to be all right, little one. I bet you're hungry. Once we're down from here, I'll get you food and water. Then you can go home with Ms. Shale. She's the best. You're gonna love her so much."

Tater Tot mews at this, as if she already knows that Ms. Shale is the best. That this is somehow common knowledge among people and cats alike. Then, something amazing happens. Tater Tot takes a tentative step near me. My fingers are right at the tip of her nose, and she takes her time smelling them. Then, she inches forward. Maybe Tater Tot wants out of this tree as much as we want to get her out. She takes another step forward, and I tell her how much she's going to love her new home. And how brave she is being right now. She scoots closer to me, and I scratch behind her ears.

My family is silent below, letting this process take as much time as I need it to take. Instead of only scratching behind her ears, I pet her whole back, and she purrs back at me.

She knows she's safe. She understands I'm trying to help her. With calm movements, I pick her up and put her in my jacket. I zip my jacket so she fits snug against me and I can use two hands to get us both down safely.

Trevor and Dad hold the ladder as I creep down its rungs. Tater Tot purrs against my chest.

We all go inside and get Tater Tot food and water. She ignores us as she gobbles her food. Ms. Shale comes in and hugs me so tight I can't breathe. "You found her!"

My face hurts from smiling so big, but this is the best day. Everyone is talking and celebrating at once.

During the commotion, I sneak back to the car and get the gift for Ms. Shale from my backpack. Nervously, I hand it to her. "This is for being a great teacher."

She opens it and gasps. "This drawing made me fall in love with that sweet kitten. Now I get to take both the drawing and the kitten home! All because of you!"

She hugs me again and whispers that I'm her favorite student, but I've got to keep that a secret. I say bye to Tater Tot. I'll miss the mischievous kitten, but she's got a great home now.

I ask Dad if I can check on Wilma before we go. We lost track of Mom at some point, but we find her in Wilma's enclosure, with Wilma sitting on her lap. They're having a full conversation with Wilma meowing to everything Mom says.

Dad looks at me. "Oh, no."

Trevor bursts out laughing. "You gonna tell her no, Dad? I think they bonded."

Dad repeats, "Oh no," but this time he's chuckling. Dad didn't want a kitten running around the house, acting crazy, not when he works from home. But Wilma isn't a kitten. She's sweet and calm. She loves napping.

"Dad, Wilma's ten years old. This is probably the most active she'll be. Ever."

He rubs his beard. "Well, I didn't know what to get your mom for Christmas."

Trevor frowns. "You know tomorrow is Christmas Eve, right?"

Dad throws an arm around Trevor and me. "Soon, I'll need to start shopping."

My arms slide around his waist. I smile up at him and then over to Mom and Wilma. "I don't think you do."

Dad says we can adopt Wilma. A giant group hug occurs. I'm not sure my mom's ever been this happy. I text Veronica and tell her the good news: Both cats have a home now, and she doesn't have to hurry back.

As we make our way back to the car, Trevor bumps his shoulder into mine. "I'm so proud of you. You never gave up or lost hope." He shakes his head. "I can't believe I almost missed all of this!"

"Christmas Eve movie marathon in the loft tomorrow night?" I grin.

"Wouldn't miss it."

About the Author

While **Desi Stowe** officially started writing in early 2022, she'd been developing her scaffolding as a writer for many years as she worked to combine her experience in healthcare and her love of writing. She has published three novels and three short stories. She lives in Raleigh, North Carolina, with her husband and two children. During the day, she works as a physical therapist. Her writing has been in sporadic spurts while juggling other responsibilities. Desi often finds herself daydreaming about plot progression and character arcs while working out or washing dishes. The characters of her written works have a special place in her heart and hopefully the readers' as well.

You can follow Desi on Instagram at:
    @desistowe
To learn more about Desi, visit her website at:
    www.desistoweauthor.com

When the Snow Settles

When the Snow Settles

Kate Ormand

December 20

The taxi slowed to a stop on Ponderosa Boulevard, tires flattening the snow.

Ember took off her headphones as she peered out the rear window at the house she'd grown up in. A house she hadn't seen in two years.

She was fifteen when her mom's car backed out of the driveway for the last time, their belongings piled in the backseat. They were about to trade their small-town life in Pine Edge, Portland, for busy city life in L.A. Ember had sat in the passenger seat with tears building in her eyes, waving goodbye to her brother, Harvey. He was ten years older than Ember, an adult when she was still a kid, but despite that, they'd been close then and still were.

Growing up, Harvey had taken Ember trick-or-treating, he'd driven her and her friends to the movies, he'd been to her school fairs. And even though they still talked all the time, Ember only saw Harvey now when he flew out to visit her and her mom in L.A., and during the one weekend a month they each spent with their dad in San Francisco. Dad had also left not long after her parents had broken the news of their divorce.

Their parents had agreed to sell the house to Harvey and his partner, Warren, and to both find their own place. Ember hadn't thought that they'd both leave Pine Edge entirely, though. Her dad, she could understand, as he'd grown up in a city and seemed drawn to the buzz of a busy life over a sleepy town, but her mom had always loved their neighborhood and the life they'd had.

Ember brought herself back to the Pine Edge of the present. She climbed out of the taxi, and the driver helped her get her suitcase from the trunk. She pulled her puffer jacket closer at the neck against the bite of the chilly winter air.

"Thank you," she said to the driver, taking her bag from him and dragging it up the path to the house. Over her shoulder, she saw the taxi pull away from the curb and caught a glimpse of the house across the street where her friend, Nolan, lived with his parents. His bedroom faced the street, but the blinds were closed.

The houses on her street were spaced apart and all of a similar style, all an assortment of painted wood and white-framed windows. The snow had covered the lupines growing on either side of her—or, more accurately now, her brother's—porch steps. Ember awaited the familiar creek of the first wooden step, but she realized they'd been replaced.

The once-green front door had been painted black, and Ember found herself raising her hand to knock on it for the first time. This wasn't her house anymore; it belonged to Harvey and Warren.

Ember's mom had left so suddenly when the town, the house, the life they once had all became too painful for her to stay. There was no scandal, no drama—her parents had drifted apart and moved on with their lives. But Ember and Harvey were left in the middle, and Ember was still figuring out how she felt.

The front door opened, spilling yellow light onto the snow.

"Hey, Bear!" Harvey pulled her into a tight hug. His familiar embrace made Ember feel slightly more at home.

He stepped back, brushing light curls from his forehead.

"Hey, Harv. The house looks great," she said, taking in all the changes. The polished wood floor, the black staircase, the large, distressed rug. Plants dotted the windowsills and artwork hung on the walls—she spotted some of her own and a hint of a smile tugged at her lips. Everything was stylish and new and nothing like she remembered.

Harvey followed her gaze. "How are you feeling? Being back here."

Their eyes met. "Strange," Ember admitted. "But okay."

Harvey stepped around Ember, heaving her suitcase over the threshold and shutting out the cold. "This is heavy for a week's stay."

"Full of gifts." Ember smirked over her shoulder.

Harvey chuckled softly. "I'll stop complaining then."

Ember hung her coat and slipped off her boots before following Harvey to the kitchen. "Hot chocolate?" he asked.

"Thanks," Ember said, sitting at a navy suede barstool. "Is Warren home?"

"He stayed late at the bar." Harvey set out two mugs on the counter. "We still have some last-minute details to take care of."

Harvey and Warren had opened a bar called Edge on Main Street. The space was previously a used bookstore, but the owner, Kit, had retired. The bookshop had been there as long as Ember could remember and the whole town knew Kit.

Ember had only seen photos of Edge, but could see that Harvey and Warren had kept a lot of the cozy bookstore feel, with low lights, mismatched furniture, and patterned wallpaper. She couldn't wait to visit in person. So far, they'd hosted holiday parties for local businesses, but were preparing for their launch party on Christmas Eve before opening officially after Christmas.

Harvey placed a steaming mug of hot chocolate in front of Ember. It was getting late, and she felt groggy from the airport. "Is it okay if I take this with me and turn in early?"

"Of course." He went to retrieve her bag as she headed for the stairs.

"Am I in my old room?"

Harvey bit his lip. "That's our office now." Ember felt her stomach sink a little. "My old room is the guest room, but I thought Mom would prefer that to staying in Dad's old study?"

Ember cleared her throat and nodded in agreement. "Okay, no problem." She couldn't blame Harvey for changing the layout of the house; it was *his* house now. Of course it would be different. Of course he'd want it to be different. And of course he wouldn't keep her room. Yet disappointment lingered alongside a feeling of loss.

Harvey took Ember's bags through to what used to be their dad's study at the back of the house downstairs. It'd been turned into a small seating room. The windows overlooked the garden, and a glass sliding door led out to the back porch, which was covered in snow and too cold to use.

The sofa bed had been made up for her, and there was a small bathroom across the hall and under the stairs with a shower, sink, and toilet.

"Do you have everything you need?" Harvey asked.

"I think so."

"Okay, great." Harvey held the door handle and backed out, slowly closing the door as he went. "It's good to have you home, Bear. Good-night." The door clicked shut.

Home, Ember thought. Where was her home?

When Ember first moved to L.A., she'd thrown herself into her art, working through numerous sketchbooks, but nothing felt right. She hadn't drawn anything in months now, lacking inspiration in an unfamiliar place. She always felt like she'd left behind a piece of herself in Pine Edge.

She unzipped her case, pulling out her pajamas and toiletries. She laid out her sketchbook and the two books she was reading on the coffee table beside an armchair. She stood for a moment in the empty room, not happy but not sad either. She could hear Harvey in the kitchen and focused on the familiarity of the sound. Ember closed her eyes and took a deep breath. Maybe she did feel like she was home.

December 21

Ember followed the scent of waffles and coffee to the kitchen.

She'd woken up early and showered, dressing in jeans and an oversized sweater. She'd opted to tie up her blonde hair in a messy bun and was wearing a pair of socks her mom had knitted for her.

"What's all this?" Ember asked, taking in the plates of waffles, fruit, eggs, bacon and toast.

"Nolan's coming over this morning," Harvey said, shuffling more toast onto a plate. Ember thought back to looking up at Nolan's bedroom window when she arrived. She'd meant to text him but had fallen asleep so quickly once she was in bed.

Ember set her empty mug from the night before by the kitchen sink. "Oh, and here I was thinking you'd done all this for me."

Harvey straightened. "I did!" He grabbed a clean mug from the cupboard. "Coffee?"

"Thanks." She sat at the same barstool and grabbed an empty plate. "What time will Nolan be here?"

"Any minute," Harvey said, glancing at her.

Ember took a sip of her coffee and focused on filling her plate. She wouldn't let Harvey see her flustered over Nolan. Though, out of the corner of her eye, she could see him fighting a smile. Nolan had always lived across the street from them. He had black hair, dark eyes, and a skateboard tucked under his arm ninety percent of the time. They'd thankfully kept in touch since Ember left Pine Edge.

Ember's best friend, Mina, kept her updated on Nolan, too. Ember always felt a stab of longing when she heard about their lives in Pine Edge while she was in L.A. She hadn't made the effort to make friends in L.A., preferring the familiarity of her friends back in Pine Edge. Even though she always had Mina and Nolan to talk to, she was lonely being so far away from them.

There was a knock at the door.

"I'll get it!" Warren called out on his way down the stairs. He paused as he passed the kitchen. "Ember!" He hurriedly hugged her before rushing to the front door. "So good to see you," he finished over his shoulder.

"You too," she called back. "How are things at Edge?"

Her question went unanswered when Nolan entered the kitchen ahead of Warren. His dark hair was tousled and a little color stood out on his pale cheeks. "You're back," he said with a wide smile.

She hopped off the barstool as Nolan approached for a hug. His signature sandalwood scent and the warmth radiating off his hoodie were two things she missed about Pine Edge the most.

Nolan glanced at the food. "Harvey! All this for me?"

"All this for *Ember*," he corrected with a laugh. Warren walked around the kitchen island, wrapping his arms around Harvey from behind. "But don't get used to it," Harvey added, resting a hand on Warren's arm. "You can have cereal tomorrow."

Ember's lips curled into a smile. "Deal."

When the four of them were full from breakfast, Ember and Nolan helped tidy up the kitchen before donning coats and boots, scarves and gloves, and heading out into the snow. The roads were cleared enough to drive on, but Ember was glad the journey to Edge was short.

Mina couldn't make it to breakfast because she'd been at choir practice, so she was meeting them at the bar.

As Warren slowly backed out of the driveway, Ember pulled out her phone to text her mom. The signal was weak, probably due to the weather, but the text sent. Her mom was a wedding photographer and had a final booking today.

"How does it feel being home again?" Nolan asked as the two of them sat together in the backseat.

"It's been good," she replied and realized she meant it. Other than the initial discomfort of seeing the house and remembering the day they left, she'd felt some familiarity seeping back in and found herself clinging to the comfort in that more than anything.

As Warren parked, Ember caught sight of Mina standing outside the bar. She was tucked under an alcove with her hands stuffed into her pockets and her chin nestled beneath the collar of her coat. When Mina saw the car, she lifted her head, smiled, and waved. She had dark skin, blue-framed glasses, and dark curls tucked under a neon-pink beanie.

Ember rushed to her best friend as fast as the snow-covered

ground would allow and pulled her into a tight hug. "I missed you!" Mina smelled like she always did, which Ember placed as lavender and jasmine, but she'd never been entirely sure. Mina's mom was a florist, and Mina worked there on the weekends, so there was always a mixture of floral scents wafting off her hair and clothes.

"Don't the two of you speak every day?" Harvey teased, coming up behind them.

"Hi, guys." Mina looked past Ember to greet Harvey, Warren, and Nolan. "I can't wait to see inside."

Edge had two large windows on either side of the door. Ember could make out some of the window seats, but the interior was cloaked in darkness.

Warren put his key in the lock and opened the door, holding it for them as they filed inside out of the cold.

Last time Ember had stepped inside the building had been two years ago when it was Kit's bookstore. It still held that leather and paper smell that would likely never go away, infused into the wooden floorboards beneath her feet.

Warren ducked behind the bar and flicked some switches, lighting the room with a soft glow.

"Wow," Ember whispered.

Spotlights framed the bar and lit up the booths, highlighting mismatched seating in various patterns and materials, wooden tables with tea lights in the center, and an array of hanging plants, tall plants, and succulents around the space. The mirrors behind the bar caught the light from the windows, making the room seem bigger than it was, though still trapping in that cozy-bookstore feel.

Ember and her friends were silent as they took it all in. She could feel Harvey's eyes on them as her face cracked a huge smile. "Wow," she said again, louder this time. "It looks incredible in here."

Harvey slung his arm over Warren's shoulder. "Thanks, Bear. That means a lot to us."

"So what can we do to get Edge ready for its grand opening?" Ember unzipped her coat, hanging it on a rack by the door with her scarf and gloves stuffed in the pocket.

"We've got a glassware delivery coming today and there's boxes of alcohol that need unpacking and putting on the shelves behind the bar." Warren grabbed his iPad. "Take a seat at one of the booths while I check over the contents, then we'll put you to work."

Nolan and Mina hung their coats with Ember's and the three of them slid into a window booth. Harvey went into the back to make coffee for everyone while Warren worked through the boxes behind the bar.

"This place really is amazing," Mina said. "You must be so proud of them."

"I am," Ember replied, sitting a little taller. "Are your parents coming to the launch party?"

"Mine are," Mina said.

"Mom's flying in tomorrow so they'll both be there," Nolan said. His mom was a flight attendant, so it wasn't unusual for her to be out of town, even around Christmas.

Harvey brought out a tray of coffees, stopping to give Warren his first.

"Our mom is too," Ember said as Harvey approached their table. She checked her phone as everyone took a coffee cup and thanked Harvey.

Nolan raised his eyebrows. "It'll be her first time back here, too, right?"

Ember blew on the edge of her cup and nodded. "How long has your mom been away this time, Nolan?" she asked. "Does she still leave you gifts when she's gone?"

"A week this time, and yeah, she still does that," Nolan said, glancing down at his hands.

"What's this?" Mina asked. "I don't think I know about this?"

"My mom gives me a gift each day she's away. It's not always a physical object. It can be anything from a voice note or a photo or a small trinket from her trip, or she'd leave something behind for me to find. It was something she started doing to let me know she was thinking of me even when she wasn't here."

Mina smiled widely. "That's so sweet, I never knew that."

Nolan shrugged.

Mina looked between the two of them. "We should make our own tradition like that in the three days leading up to Christmas. Because even if we're not all together, it would still work from a distance."

Ember thought about it for a moment. Starting a Christmas tradition between the three of them would ensure she still held a piece of her life in Pine Edge even if she was celebrating Christmas in L.A.

"Okay," Ember said, and Nolan nodded in agreement.

Mina clapped her hands. "Great. I'll do the twenty-second, Nolan can take the twenty-third, and Ember can do Christmas Eve. This will be fun!"

"The delivery is coming in now," Warren called over. The three of them finished their coffees and went to help.

December 22

Holiday movies played in the background while Ember and Warren decorated the Christmas tree, and Harvey baked his white chocolate, cranberry, and orange cookies in the kitchen. Ember had missed out on those cookies for the past two years, for the two Christmases they'd spent apart.

"We're usually a December first kind of household when it comes to decorating," Warren said, riffling through a cardboard box of decorations. It still contained all the ones from Ember and Harvey's childhood, with a few new additions.

"Us too. We may have crept into November a couple of times." Ember laughed. "But we'll let you off this year while you've had a lot going on."

Warren put his hand over his heart. "Very kind of you." He cleared his throat. "But, in all seriousness I do hope we've done the right thing."

Ember hung a bauble and twisted it into place. "Edge is going to be a success," she predicted. "You've hosted half the town's Christmas parties before officially opening. They're there for you. We all are."

Warren nodded, reassured. "You're right," he said, offering a hint of a smile before turning back toward the box of ornaments.

Ember's phone buzzed with a text from her mom. She'd replied yesterday to confirm everything was going ahead and she was due to fly in today, but her latest text informed Ember her flight had been canceled due to the weather.

"No," Ember groaned. "Mom's flight is delayed."

Ember was missing her mom. In L.A., it was just the two of them. Neither of them had much of a social life. Even though her parents' divorce had been civilized, Ember still sensed a shift in her mom. Like she wasn't as quick to trust or take chances. She focused on her work and not much else. When they lived in Pine Edge, they'd both been so busy all the time. Though it was nice to have grown closer and have more time for each other, their world was small in L.A., and Ember kept thinking of her mom alone so close to Christmas.

Warren stepped toward her. "Until when?"

Ember took a deep breath as she read on. "Tomorrow morning." She looked out at the weather. "If it stops snowing." She put the ornament she was holding back in the box. "I'm going to let Harvey know," she said, and headed toward the kitchen.

Ember obsessively checked her phone and the weather app up until Nolan and Mina came over later in the day. She told them what had happened, and Nolan said his mom was delayed, too.

Her spirits were lifted as Warren handed out blankets and Harvey handed out cookies and they all settled on the sofas to watch a movie.

Ember sat between Nolan and Mina. "I have your gifts for today to kick off our new tradition," Mina declared before the movie began. "I got you both a memory."

Nolan and Ember glanced at each other before turning to face Mina. "Nolan, I'll start with you." She smiled at him. "The first football game after Ember moved away, you came with me in her place because you knew it was something Ember and I always did. I know you don't like football and you don't like the games, but you came with me anyway and I'm not sure if I told you how much I appreciated you for that." Nolan smiled and nodded once.

Mina placed her hand over Ember's.

"Ember, when my family moved here, I was twelve and kind of terrified of starting at school. I'd never moved before, and in the movies you always see the new kid either thriving or surviving, and I was not ready for that. I felt lost and alone, and it was nothing like the movies." She laughed. Ember laughed, too, knowing what Mina was going to say next.

"When you turned around in the lunch line and knocked my soda out of my hand, soaking both our shoes—that was movie-worthy." She smiled widely. "I'm glad you bumped into me that day."

Ember turned her hand over and squeezed Mina's. "Me too."

When everyone had gone home, Ember wandered upstairs to her old room.

The house was quiet, all but for the hum of the television Harvey and Warren had fallen asleep in front of. Ember's memories were swirling in her head.

She pushed open the door and felt for the switch, clicking on the overhead light.

The room followed the same decor as the rest of the house, with a dark wooden desk by the window, a tall plant beside it, and a navy chair with a gold frame. Bookshelves lined one wall, an armchair with a crochet blanket draped over the back of it sat at an angle beside a floor lamp.

Ember stood for a moment in a room that was familiar but not.

She'd expected to feel sadness coming in here, but she didn't. She recognized the room wasn't hers anymore, but the life she left behind was still within reach. With her friends and her brother and Warren—and soon, her mom—she was right where she wanted to be. Being back made her miss her dad, too, but she'd gotten used to missing him over the past two years. It was only just hitting her how much she'd missed *this*.

Coming back to Pine Edge, she'd wanted to step back into the past and for everything to be the same, but she was now realizing it was okay for things to be a little different. Everything that really mattered wasn't going anywhere. It'd been waiting here for her all along.

Ember went downstairs to retrieve the sketchpad and pencils from her room and brought them back to the study. She sat at the desk and began to draw.

December 23

Edge was bustling with activity. Warren was training staff, distributing uniforms, and perfecting the final details ahead of their launch party.

Harvey was in the kitchen with the cooks, and Ember, Mina, and Nolan sat folding napkins, stacking menus, and polishing glasses.

"The food looks good," Nolan said. The menu was small but there was a good selection. "I'll see if I can get us all some lunch."

Nolan slid out of the booth as Ember watched the snow fall outside the bar. Mina followed her gaze. "Have you heard from your mom?" she asked.

"Delayed again," Ember sighed. "I'm getting worried now that she won't make it in time for Christmas."

Live music filled the bar before Ember had a chance to think more about it. She recognized the Green Day song right away. Her eyes found the source. Nolan was standing beside the DJ booth, a guitar in hand. From the corner of her eye, she could see Mina look between her and Nolan, but Ember didn't shift her gaze from him for the whole song. He played "Wake Me up When September Ends," knowing Green Day was Ember's favorite band. This must be his gift to them.

The busy bar had paused to watch him and applauded as he finished playing. He set down his guitar and made his way back to the table. Ember and Mina were still clapping when he reached them.

Ember's heart raced in her chest, her words lodged in her throat.

"Hey, Nolan?" Mina teased, saving Ember from having to think in a moment she was still processing. "Where's our lunch?"

Nolan laughed. "Right!" he said, spinning on his heel and heading into the kitchen.

"I'm so glad we did this," Mina giggled.

As the day moved into evening, Mina left for a choir performance at the retirement center where her grandma lived.

Nolan offered to walk Ember home, as Harvey and Warren were still so busy. They gathered up their coats, hats, and gloves, and set out into the snow. It'd finally stopped coming down, at least. The town was quiet: people settled inside their homes, smoke rose from fireplace chimneys, and fairy lights sparkled as the pink-tinged sky darkened overhead.

Ember stuffed her gloved hands into her pockets. "Your gift was so great," she said. "We loved it."

Nolan smirked, looking down at his feet. "Glad you liked it."

"Weren't you nervous?" she asked. "Playing for everyone."

"I wasn't playing for everyone," he said softly.

Ember glanced at him and then looked away. "Have you heard from your mom?" she asked.

"Yeah. She's delayed, too, but the snow stopping is a good sign." He looked up at the sky. "Maybe they'll make it home in time."

"I hope so," Ember whispered.

They waited to cross the road as car tires crunched down the street.

"Did Harvey tell you he invited my dad and me over for Christmas?" Ember nodded.

"Great," he said. "We're a little useless without Mom."

"Neither of you cook?" Ember asked, stepping around an icy patch.

"We cook, but we're not organized when it comes to shopping for food."

Ember grinned. "Harvey is looking forward to cooking for everyone. It'll be great."

When they reached their houses, Nolan waited until Ember had unlocked the front door and gone inside. She waved in the doorway as he turned to cross the street to his own house.

Ember took off her boots and coat and went back to the upstairs study, to the sketchpads she'd left on the desk.

December 24

One hour until the launch party for Edge, and the staff was busy turning on LED candles and setting up for opening. Ember knew in an hour the bar would be packed. The turnout to support a local business was always huge in Pine Edge. It was one of the things she'd loved so much about living there.

She ran her hands down the all-black uniform. The door opened and Ember turned to see who'd arrived early.

"Mom!" she squealed, clearing the few steps between them and pulling her into a tight hug. "You're here!"

"I went by the house, then figured you'd all be here."

Ember swallowed. "I'm sorry, Mom. I haven't been checking my phone as much as I should've." She'd been so busy helping set up the bar that her phone had sat in her pocket mostly forgotten.

"That's okay, honey. I know how busy you've all been." She looked around. "I'm just glad I get to experience this with you both. The bar looks incredible."

Ember beamed. "It's amazing. Actually, I wanted to speak to you about—"

"Mom, you made it!" Harvey rushed out of the kitchen, arms wide to embrace her.

She held on to him. "I'm so proud of you," Mom said into Harvey's shoulder. She stepped back, still clasping Harvey's arms. "It's going to be a big hit."

"We've got an hour until we open the doors," he said, noting the suitcase behind their mom. "Do you want to go back to the house with your bags or leave them in the back here?"

"I can come back with you, Mom," Ember offered.

Their mom waved them both off. "Don't worry. It wasn't too long a flight. I'll freshen up here and take a look at your cocktail menu."

Harvey tilted his head and gestured toward the bar. Mom followed him, and Ember wheeled the suitcase into the back storeroom.

Once her mom was situated at the bar, Ember joined her while Warren made Mom's drink.

"Tell me," her mom said, "how's it been, being back here?"

Ember bit at the skin on her lip. "That's what I wanted to talk to you about," she began. "It was difficult when I first arrived at the house but now . . . I want to stay," she said quietly.

Mom shifted in her seat.

"I'm sorry if it's painful to hear," Ember said quickly. The last thing she wanted to do was hurt her mom. "I've just found it such a comfort being back."

"And you haven't been reminded too much of our life here before the divorce?"

"Yes," Ember said. "I have, but they're good memories. And I've made new ones, too, in the time I've been back. I've been happy here, and you being here now just makes it better."

Mom took a sip of her drink.

"You only just got here," Ember continued. "I don't expect you to feel the same way, but maybe if you have an open mind—"

She put down her drink. "Ember," she said softly, shaking her head. "I don't know. My marriage ended here."

Ember smiled sadly. "Your family started here, too."

Mom sighed gently and looked down at her lap. "Let's enjoy this Christmas together. Then we'll see."

"We will," Ember said, disappointed but understanding.

Ember stood and her mom reached for her arm, stopping her. "I can admit, being back feels different from how I thought it would.

And I do sometimes wonder if moving to L.A. was . . . a mistake." She paused. "I just need to think about it, okay?"

Ember nodded. "Okay."

As predicted, an hour later, the bar was packed.

Ember and Mina walked around the room serving bite-sized samples from the menu. Ember carried a tray of soft pretzel bites, which she'd had to refill twice already. Mina had mozzarella sticks and goats' cheese balls, which seemed to be a big hit, too. All booths, tables, and barstools were full. People stood around in groups, drinks in hand, taking from the trays of food circling the room.

The bar was busy, the kitchen was busy, music played, and the space was abuzz with conversation. The floor was a sea of festive sweaters, with fairy lights twinkling around the room—the atmosphere was exactly as Ember had pictured it.

Kit, the former owner of the bookstore, sat at the end of the bar. She looked proud, taking it all in with an Old Fashioned nestled between her hands. Ember only knew that drink because her dad liked it. She wondered what he'd make of it all. She was sure he'd love to come and see it some time.

Nolan arrived with both his parents, nudging through the crowd to reach Ember. He had a huge smile on his face. His mom waved to Ember the moment she saw her. "It's so good to have you back, Ember!" she said. "Is your mom here?"

Ember pointed to the booth where her mom sat catching up with Mina's mom and other friends. Nolan's mom made her way over to their table and his dad went to the bar to get their drinks. Nolan stayed beside Ember. "I'm glad your mom made it home," she said to him.

"I'm glad yours did, too."

"You're still coming over for Christmas, right?"

He nodded. "It's too late to change our plans now. Plus, we're all looking forward to it."

Ember smiled at him. Her tray was empty, and she held it at her side. She'd need to go back to the kitchen to fill up. "Us too," she said.

Nolan noted the tray, gesturing to it. "I'll let you get back to work. I'll see if Harvey needs help with anything."

It was close to midnight when Ember and her mom walked arm-in-arm up to the door of their old house. Harvey and Warren were still at Edge and weren't sure what time they'd be home.

"It's changed inside," Ember warned as she put the key into the lock. "But it looks great," she added.

Mom gasped under her breath as she stepped inside. "I have to admit it does look good," she agreed, surveying the photos on the walls.

"You're staying in Harvey's old room," Ember told her mom. "My old room is an office now. I've been sketching in there."

Mom tilted her head. "Where are you sleeping?"

Ember swallowed. "I'm in Dad's old study."

Mom nodded. "Will you help me bring my bags up?"

Ember gestured toward the staircase and her mom headed up, Ember following with the suitcase. The stairs were narrow. She glanced toward her old room as they passed, the door open a crack and the room in darkness. Harvey's old room was to their right, and Mom pushed the door open and went in first. She clicked on the reading light beside the bed as Ember stepped in. The ceiling slanted, the queen bed against the far end of the room. A nightstand on either side. Ember wheeled the suitcase up to the foot of the bed.

"This is cozy," Mom said, sitting on the edge of the mattress.

Ember sat beside her and linked her arm through her mom's, resting her head on her shoulder. "How're you finding everything so far?" she asked.

"Better than expected," Mom said. She kissed the top of Ember's head. "Let's see some of those sketches?"

December 25

On Christmas morning, Ember knocked on her mom's bedroom door with a mug of coffee in hand.

"Come in," Mom called.

Ember entered the room, finding the bed made and Mom sitting on top of the covers wrapping gifts.

"Last-minute wrapping," she admitted.

Ember set the mug down on the bedside table. "Happy Christmas, Mom," she said, leaning over to wrap an arm around her.

"Happy Christmas, honey. Thank you for the coffee."

Ember sat on the edge of the mattress. "Did you sleep well?"

"Really well," she said. "It was great catching up with Jodie and the others last night. Do you know they still have the book club going?"

Jodie was Nolan's mom, and together they'd started up a book club before she and Ember had moved away.

"Fifteen members," she said, eyebrows raised. "Seems like they have a ball."

Ember laughed at the hint of jealousy in her mom's voice. "It sounds great. Will you be able to catch one before we leave?"

"I don't think so," she sighed. "We have to be back before New Year's."

Ember's stomach dropped at the reminder that their stay here wasn't permanent. It felt like it should be.

"Mom," she began, pausing to take a breath. "I meant what I said last night. I really do miss it here. I *really* want to stay."

The Gift Exchange

Mom twisted around to pick up her coffee mug. "I thought you might." She took a sip. "It wasn't you who decided to leave town in the first place. I'm sorry if I caused you to think your feelings about Pine Edge needed to match mine in any way."

Ember shook her head. "Mom, no, that's not it. I felt it too when I first got here. I missed our family being together, living in this house, and I was reminded how it felt when we split apart. But then there's this conflicting feeling of belonging and home that keeps growing. And I don't feel that in L.A."

"Me neither," Mom whispered. "It's a lot to think about still. Can you give me some time to talk to your brother, too?"

Ember felt hope spark in her chest.

Mina and Nolan arrived at the house midmorning, after Ember had opened gifts with her mom, brother, and Warren. Harvey was now busy in the kitchen, and Mom and Warren were lending a hand.

"Happy Christmas!" Mina cheered, handing Ember a wrapped parcel. Ember handed one back. Ember unwrapped a new sketchbook, while Mina unwrapped a hardcover book.

Nolan cleared his throat. "I didn't know we were doing gifts."

"That's okay," Mina said. "Your song was enough." She turned to Ember. "Speaking of . . . you didn't give us your gift yesterday!"

Ember had completely forgotten in the buzz of the Edge launch party. "I have them upstairs," she said, dashing off to retrieve the sketches she'd made of them.

When she returned, she handed them to both Mina and Nolan at the same time. In one, Mina was standing in the center surrounded by flowers. In the other, Nolan rode his skateboard, his hood raised.

"Wow," they both said in unison. Mina added, "They're amazing, Ember."

Ember felt her cheeks heat at the compliment. "Thanks," she said. "I rushed them, but they turned out okay."

They both thanked her again, then the three of them offered their help in the kitchen. When they were turned away, they sat together on the sofa until Mina had to rejoin her own family and Nolan's parents arrived for dinner.

Ember and Nolan set the table while Harvey and Warren brought out all the food. A turkey sat in the middle of the table, surrounded by bowls of mashed potatoes, cranberry sauce, stuffing, gravy, and vegetables.

Everyone joined around the table and filled their plates. Conversation flowed easily about the bar, their parents' jobs, the book club, school, and life in Pine Edge. Ember paused and took a deep breath. In that moment, she felt like she was exactly where she should be.

After dinner, Ember's mom pulled her to the side. "Can we have a quick chat?"

Ember followed her mom through to the kitchen. Everyone else remained talking at the dinner table while pecan pie was in the oven for dessert.

"I've spoken with your brother," Mom said, perching on one of the barstools. "He said if we want to move back here that we can make it work."

Ember's eyebrows shot up. "Here? In this house?"

Her mom shook her head. "This house is Harvey and Warren's," she said. "They've invited us to live here a short time while we find our own place, but—"

Ember threw herself at her mom, wrapping her arms around her in a tight hug.

"Thank you, thank you," she said. "I can't believe this!"

Ember's mom squeezed her back. "It's a lot to consider," she said.

"But we've done it once, so we can do it again. I spoke to the girls last night and they tried to convince me to come back, too. Lots of weddings I can work here, and you'll be able to slot back in at school. . . ." Mom trailed off in her thoughts.

Ember stepped back. "I can't wait to tell Mina."

"Let's just take it one step at a time." Noticing Ember's disappointment, she added, "But you can go ahead and tell Mina and Nolan, if you want to."

"Does this mean we don't have to leave by New Year's?"

"I need a little more time to say for sure, and I do have to go back for the weddings I'm booked for. But you can stay here." She brushed Ember's hair off her forehead. "We're not in a rush to return other than to finalize some things and pack up."

Ember breathed a sigh of relief. "I still can't believe we're doing this."

"I want to bring my family back together." She rubbed Ember's arm. "I know now that we belong here. It didn't take me long to realize that. I needed to leave at the time, but I'm sorry for everything I've put you through."

"You don't need to apologize, Mom."

"I uprooted you suddenly, taking you away from your friends and your brother," Mom said. "When your dad and I split, even though it was the right choice for us and we didn't part on unfriendly terms, accepting that that chapter of my life was over still struck me hard."

Ember nodded. "It was hard," she agreed.

Mom took her hand. "At the time, I felt like I needed a fresh start away from Pine Edge to let everything settle in my mind." She looked at Ember and smiled sadly. "I noticed you'd stopped drawing. You didn't make friends, and you asked me if we could come back to Pine Edge, and I just buried myself in my work because I didn't know what to do."

"It's okay to make mistakes," Ember reassured.

Mom blinked away tears. "You stopped asking to come back."

"I got scared, too," Ember whispered. "I didn't know how I would feel either. The longer we were away, coming back seemed even scarier." She shrugged. "I was only talking to Mina and Nolan long distance, hearing about their lives back here and I wanted to be part of it, but wasn't sure I had a place anymore."

"You always have a place here."

Ember nodded. "I know that now."

They hugged again, wiped their eyes, and took their seats at the table as Harvey announced that dessert was ready to serve.

The world outside was quiet, the sky darkening and the snow settling as afternoon shifted to evening. The final board game was played, and Nolan's family stood to leave.

"Thank you for hosting," Jodie said to Harvey and Warren. She turned to Ember's mom and placed a hand on her shoulder. "I'm so pleased everything worked out." The two of them then launched into another conversation, sharing ideas of where Ember and her mom could live.

Realizing they may be a while longer, Ember followed Nolan out onto the quiet street. "I can't believe you're staying," he said, his breath visible in the crisp air. "It's the best gift."

Ember smiled widely. "I know. It's a shame we won't be neighbors though." She looked up at the house. "I have one more gift for you."

She took his hand in hers, leaned forward, paused for just a moment, and then pressed her lips to his. She felt him smile and she smiled, too, stepping back but keeping hold of his hand.

"Happy Christmas," she said softly.

About the Author

Kate Ormand is YA author of Dark Days and shape-shifter circus series, The Wanderers (winner of the USA Best Book Awards in the young adult fiction category) and The Pack. Kate lives in the UK and graduated from university with a degree in Fine Art Painting. It was during this course that Kate discovered her love of reading YA books, prompting her to try a new creative angle and experiment with writing.

You can follow Kate on Instagram at:
    @_katels

To learn more about Kate, visit her website at:
    https://kateormand.wordpress.com

The First Christmas

The First Christmas

Jessica Daniliuk

Becca had always loved the holiday season. Even though her mother was crazy about the schedule and her brother, Ian, always seemed to forget they lived in Utah and constantly complained about having to drive in the snow, she'd made some of her fondest memories during the holidays. Christmastime meant her dad would be home for a whole week; there would be no business conference in Canada to pull him away, and he'd be there for every perfectly planned-out minute.

Holidays were a well-oiled machine, making it difficult to bring just anyone into the mix. Ian's wife, Kim, was a superstar, having taken to their traditions without trying to impose any of her own. She even participated in the annual Sled Race, something that seemed rather childish but was incredibly important. Becca had always known that to preserve the traditions she adored, she'd have to find someone who was funny, kind, good at Scrabble, and had an overflowing amount of Christmas Spirit. When Becca first met Lina in middle school and later saw she dressed as Jack Skellington for Halloween, she knew she'd found The One.

They were childhood sweethearts, and many thought they were crazy for going to the same school and moving into an apartment together their first year of college, but Becca didn't see it that way. For her, Lina was her home away from home, and she couldn't have moved across the country without Lina by her side. They had been together for six years, which was considered a lifetime for people their age. Lina loved to deck the halls, was seen as part of the family, and made a mean hot chocolate, so she wasn't going anywhere. Becca couldn't be more grateful for that. Especially this year.

A mere week before Christmas Day, Becca was just hanging the last few ornaments on her Christmas tree. Christmas was her favorite holiday, but it had admittedly snuck up on her this time. She'd finish her decorating just in time to hop on a flight that would take her to her family and their planned celebrations. She'd be coming back to her apartment a few days after the twenty-fifth, but Becca still wanted to have a Christmas tree. In fact, she *needed* this tree; she hadn't had time to put up any other decorations, and it felt depressing leaving her apartment with no jolly. As she put the last ornament on the tree, Lina came up behind her and pulled her in.

"I just have one more, I swear," Becca said with a playful annoyance. "And it's a really good one. It's the Christmas pickle. Please. I promise, then I'm done."

Lina let her go; she knew not to disturb Becca in those essential moments. "Fine. But you need to finish packing, we have to leave in fifteen minutes."

Becca placed the last ornament on the tree—a camouflaged pickle—and stepped back to admire her handiwork. Their cat, Eddie, walked up to her and rubbed himself against Becca's leg.

"Seems like Eddie likes it."

"For someone who looks forward to this week every year, you sure are procrastinating getting ready."

Becca turned to meet Lina's eyes. She was right. Becca had only done half the packing she needed to. She still had to put all of the gifts in a bag, make sure Eddie's things were together, and coax him into the cat carrier. She didn't feel ready for this year, and not just because she'd waited so long to set up her tree. It felt like she was outside her body, watching a crazed woman go through the motions. Nothing had been right since October; even things she enjoyed, like writing, had become tiresome. She'd barely made it through the first semester of school, and even though everyone understood why, she still felt like a failure. She wanted to be the hero everyone needed. She knew this was an important Christmas, and she wanted to be there for her family, but her feet were glued to the floor and she had no motivation to unstick them. How was she supposed to do this with her dad gone?

Lina started putting all of Eddie's essentials in a bag. Lina's mother cared even more about sticking to a schedule, so missing their flight would be bad for Becca but detrimental for Lina. Lina walked back over to Becca, who was still staring at the tree.

"How about letting in some light? Let the neighbors see your masterpiece."

Lina pulled the curtains back to reveal a wall of white. A sheet of snow made it so Becca could not see even the tallest skyscraper. Becca watched as panic spread across Lina's face. There was no way any flight would be taking off in this.

Lina rushed over to the couch, grabbed the remote, and turned on the TV. Every channel was chronicling the impending storm, the worst one New York would have seen in over a decade. Within a few minutes, Becca's phone buzzed with a notification from the airline: "All flights will be delayed indefinitely due to dangerous weather conditions."

Relief washed over Becca, which made her feel guilty. Becca walked over to the couch and sat down next to Lina, who was frantically flipping through channels, trying to find a different outcome, one that would get them on that flight.

Becca gently placed her hand on Lina's, signaling for her to put the remote down. Lina listened, turning off the TV and facing Becca on the couch. Becca desperately wanted to say something, but her throat was as frozen as New York. She slowly rose off the couch and walked into the bedroom, barely listening as Lina tried to call her mom.

An hour passed before Becca was able to dial the phone; they were supposed to be going through TSA at that point. She paced around her room, dreading the concept of making her mother upset. Becca chickened out twice before finally hitting the call button on the third attempt.

"Hi sweetie, everything okay? Are you at the gate?"

Becca paused for a moment, allowing everything to defrost. "I'm so sorry, Mom. I don't think Lina and I will be making it for Christmas this year." Her heart squeezed; it felt like she had willed this to happen.

Her mom sounded exhausted; everything was probably set up. "What happened? Are you guys all right?"

"Yes, we're fine. There's a massive storm right now that's keeping all flights on the ground. We don't know when it's gonna let up or if we'll be able to get on another flight, so I just wanted to let you know now. Send my love to Ian and Kim."

Becca couldn't talk to her brother; he'd find a way to make her feel bad even if he didn't mean to, and even if, deep down, she knew it wasn't her fault. She wanted the conversation to be over—something she never expected to feel talking to her mother.

"We're going to miss you so much, sweetie. " It sounded like she was about to cry, and Becca could relate.

"I love you, Mom."

"Love you too, Becca."

Becca hung up, fell onto the bed, and curled into a ball, hoping that would keep the tears from coming. It didn't work. Warm tears streamed down her cold cheeks before gently dropping to the comforter. She hadn't fully accepted but had processed the fact that she wouldn't be having Christmas with her father, but now she wouldn't be having it with her mother or brother either. Becca wouldn't be there for them during a time when they needed her most, and the guilt was beginning to paralyze her. She could hear Lina on the phone with her parents on the other side of the door, talking about how they'd have to postpone everything. Becca hadn't missed a Christmas since she was eight years old, due to a cold that had been circulating through the school since September. And even then, she was able to participate in Holiday Pictionary from her doorway.

At the thought of missing her family's frozen lasagna, Becca's breath hitched Even though Christmas celebrations were now planned to a T, they weren't always.

When Becca and her brother were younger, their mother was juggling a lot between getting everything they needed for the holiday and finding ways to keep the magic alive. Their dad always worked up until December 23, so a lot of responsibility fell on their mom. One year, she got swept up in the chaos of it all and forgot to buy a ham. Even though Ian rejoiced at the concept of eating only side dishes, their mom had been devastated and embarrassed. Becca's dad had offered to go to the grocery store the day before Christmas Eve to try and find a ham, which had calmed her down for a moment, but to nobody's surprise, the grocery store had been ransacked, and there was no ham or similar dish to bring back. Not wanting to return empty-handed, Dad made his way to the frozen aisle and grabbed the smallest box of lasagna possibly ever made. Even though it wasn't what she'd wanted, when Becca's mom saw the pitiful replacement, she'd laughed and laughed for the first time all season. This amused the others, and from that day forward, frozen lasagna became a staple on the Christmas dinner table. Kim and Lina always skipped it, so the four of them were able to continue cutting the square into perfect quarters. Imagining two slices left in the container this year was killing Becca.

As her guilt and memories of Christmases past continued to attack her, Becca lay her head on the pillow, and once the tears slowed, she closed her eyes.

Becca woke three hours later, blissfully unaware she had drifted off. She swung her feet around, eventually sliding them into her slippers after much trial and error. She trudged over to the door and pushed it open.

She rubbed the sleep out of her swollen eyes as she spoke. "Thanks for letting me sleep, love. I really needed that."

As she moved her hands away from her face, Becca was met by a Winter Wonderland. She wondered if she was still dreaming as she took in her living room, which had been transformed into the inside of a snow globe. Paper cut into the shape of snowflakes hung from the ceiling with clear wire. Every available surface was covered with garland and sparkly lights. Some of the decorations Becca made as a kid that her mom had forced her to keep had been lovingly displayed on the wall over the family photos. Mistletoe had been taped to the front doorframe, and the smell of cookies and hot chocolate was wafting in the air.

In the center of it all was Eddie wearing paper antlers on his head, akin to Max from *How the Grinch Stole Christmas*, with Lina wearing a mask of the green creature himself. Becca was confused, but for the first time in a while, she wasn't on autopilot; she was in the moment, experiencing everything. Her heart was beating fast, motivated by pure curiosity.

Lina took off the mask and walked toward Becca. "Sorry it's not the whole costume, I can only seem to find the mask."

Becca spun around, taking in the scene from every angle.

Her words felt light. "What—what is this?"

"Christmas is coming, it's practically here!" Lina did her best to sound like the Grinch. "But I heard somebody hasn't been celebrating, so we must fix that right away."

Becca couldn't help but giggle, not because she found it funny, even though the Grinch impression was *something else*, but because she couldn't believe someone loved her this much. Lina was missing time with her own family but had only thought about saving Becca's night.

"Lead the way, Mr. Grinch. Or is it just Grinch? I never understood that."

Lina continued with her impression, "Either is fine. We all know how much I hate Christmas, specifically presents. I can barely look at them, so I've hidden the gifts! You have to find them and save Christmas."

A light gasp escaped Becca. She couldn't believe Lina had remembered.

In fairness, it wasn't a complete surprise; it was in true Lina fashion to remember something Becca had only mentioned once and turn it into a grand romantic gesture.

But Becca was truly shocked by how Lina's scavenger hunt reminded Becca of one of her family's Christmas traditions that had faded over time. For a few years, Becca's parents would hide three presents around the house for the kids to find. The children looked in the fireplace, behind the couch, and even in the dog's food bowl for those treasures. One year, Dad even hid a present between the mattress and the box spring. Becca knew it was him from the way he was giggling like a kid as Ian kept missing the lump in the bed. She hoped she would never forget his laugh.

At the end of each hunt would be the biggest present of that Christmas—the one at the top of each kid's list—so for a while, it was Becca's favorite tradition. But, as the kids got older and more people were added to the family, the scavenger hunts stopped. It had been years since Becca had thought about their holiday hunts. Even if she wasn't able to participate in every tradition this year, Lina was giving her this one.

"There are five gifts in total for you to track down. If you succeed, the Whos will play their horns and sing in your honor, which will be dreadful."

Becca couldn't refrain from grinning over Lina's dedication to maintaining the Grinch's character motivations.

"Five gifts?! Lina, you didn't have to; that's too much."

Lina looked very serious as she tried to get back to the task at hand. A full-blown smile spread across Becca's face, an expression that hadn't been used in some time but was now welcome back. Becca loved a lot about Lina, and one of those things was the fact that Lina was a horrible liar. She didn't have a dishonest bone in her body, even when it came to non-malicious lies like surprises.

Becca glared at Lina for a moment and watched as she broke and glanced at Eddie's bed. Becca walked over and ripped off the blanket to find a beautiful pair of emerald earrings. A few months earlier, Becca and Lina were having a casual shopping day and came across a small boutique. Like a moth to a flame, Becca was immediately drawn to an emerald necklace. She had a strong connection to emeralds, it being her birthstone, but didn't pick up the necklace because she never typically wore them. Of course, Lina would remember that day.

Becca went to throw her arms around Lina, but Lina stopped her. "You still have four more gifts to find!"

Becca looked between the couch cushions, on top of the tall bookshelf, she even looked under the tree, thinking Lina might hide something in plain sight. As Becca made her way over to the kitchen, she could see Lina growing restless; she must've been close. Becca ripped open the cabinets above the counter, only to find old cereal boxes and granola bars. Her eyes panned down for a moment, and she noticed something reflective in the microwave. She pulled it open and discovered a small painting of Eddie as Batman. Becca put the photo down and bent over, laughing hysterically. Besides Lina, Becca had three big loves: Eddie, the microwave, and Batman; each one being a reliable source of comfort. Through the gift and presentation, Lina was able to flawlessly connect the three. Becca's intuition all those years ago was correct; Lina had mastered the art of nurturing the Christmas spirit. Lina might have been the one dressed as the Grinch, but Becca's heart was growing.

"Three left."

Becca put the photo down on the counter and continued to the bathroom. She checked in the shower, expecting something to be put in the largest spot, but there was nothing. Her mind went to a disgusting place.

"Lina, you didn't. The toilet?"

Moving at half her regular speed, Becca slowly lifted the toilet seat up and was relieved to find it completely empty. She knew they kept the toilet clean—she'd cleaned it earlier that day—but no gift was worth sticking her hand in a toilet bowl. The smell of cleaner breached her nose, causing it to run. She ripped off some toilet paper and blew her nose in a way that was *definitely* attractive. As she threw the makeshift tissue away, she realized the trash had been emptied. Becca grabbed both sides of the trash can and gently shook it, listening to something bounce around inside. She lifted up the trash bag to see a DVD collection of the Santa Clause trilogy. There was an immovable lump in Becca's throat. She couldn't believe how seen she was.

"The Grinch heard a rumor that you watch these movies every year with your fellow Grinches and thought you would like to enjoy them anytime at home."

"Lina . . ." That's all Becca could say before the lump took away her ability to speak. Tears were inevitable at that point.

Lina spoke without her Grinch persona. "You can also use my DVD player, the one that plugs right into your laptop. I honestly think I am the only person our age who still appreciates a DVD. Sorry, back in character now."

As Becca continued to stare at the DVD case, she tried to clear her throat, but it was impossibly stuck. Becca's father was the type to dress up as Santa Claus in the off chance that his children would wake up in the middle of the night to try and catch a glimpse of the real Saint Nick. He did everything he could to keep the magic alive and was so devastated when Ian stopped believing that he felt the need to pull out all the stops for Becca the next year. She was about to go to sleep when suddenly footsteps were heard right over her bed. No memory was as vivid in Becca's head as when she was eight, looking up at the roof to see a sleigh, reindeer, and Santa Claus preparing to deliver her presents. The image only solidified when Santa took the wrong step and tumbled off the roof, landing butt-first in a bank of snow. As the ambulance hauled her dad off to the hospital, Becca realized Santa wasn't real, but her dad was her hero. Shortly after that event, the first *Santa Clause* movie came out, and Becca's dad swore they got the falling-off-the-roof idea from him. So, from then on, they watched the movies every Christmas Eve to remember the magic that was always present in their household.

Looking down at the DVD made it feel like a piece of her dad was in the room. Becca went to hug Lina, but Lina stepped back.

"Almost, almost. Two left!"

Becca walked back into the living room and followed the trim around the entire space.

"Our apartment isn't that big. How am I missing this?" Becca put her hand on her hip and tried to look at the whole picture, but it was useless. She was stumped.

"You have looked under, but have we looked inside, I wonder?" Lina transferred her weight back and forth between her feet and began moving her hands into figure eights.

"Since when does The Grinch tell riddles?"

"Since I thought it would be fun." Lina was talking like a ghost. Becca had to find the other two presents soon before everything went further off the rails.

Becca crept over to the Christmas tree and looked in the direction of where she had placed the Christmas Pickle. She scanned over the branches . . . nothing. Lina was practically about to jump out of her own skin, so Becca could tell she was on the right path. While growing up, anytime Becca would struggle with a math problem, her dad would tell her to "collect herself and look at the problem with one eye." Becca spent years trying to understand what kind of metaphor that was before realizing it wasn't. Her dad just knew that looking at it with one eye shut would make her laugh and turn frustration into joy.

Like a worm, her father's voice slithered its way into her brain. Becca collected herself and closed one eye. Within the middle branches, a black baseball hat was lying perfectly on its side. Becca carefully reached in, making sure to avoid all of the baubles. On the front of the hat was a small image of Jack Skellington's face. The neck massager Becca got for Lina was beginning to look worse and worse.

Lina took a step closer and, for a second, dropped the Grinch accent. "One more."

The only place left to look was the bedroom.

"There's no way. I was in there; I would've noticed you hiding a gift."

Lina just shrugged. Becca tiptoed into the bedroom as if afraid the gift would jump out at her. She'd been in the bed; it couldn't be in there. She ran over to the closet and ripped it apart. Nothing. She threw herself to the ground to search under the bed. Nothing. She started pawing through drawers. She'd clean everything up later; she was on a mission.

"She's determined, look at her little nose scrunch."

A voice she desperately needed to hear nearly brought Becca to her knees. She looked back at Lina to see her holding up a phone. Lina turned the phone to reveal the smiling faces of Ian, Kim, and Becca's mom. Tears began to pool in the corners of both eyes, but Becca tried to keep them in; she couldn't let her family know exactly how much she was hurting.

As if she were the same age she'd been when they'd held their last holiday hunt, Becca called out for her mother: "Mom!"

She grabbed the phone from Lina's hands and was no longer able to conceal her shame. The tears were coming whether she wanted them to or not.

"I'm so sorry there will be two pieces of lasagna left." The words leapt out of her mouth before she had a chance to edit them.

Becca's mom chuckled slightly. "It's okay, darling. We will have it another time."

"But—but it's Christmas." Becca was technically an adult, but she still felt like a kid, and she needed a hug from her mother.

"Just an excuse to see you, Becks." Ian chimed in.

Hearing the nickname that only Ian called her created a warmth that wrapped around Becca like a hug.

"We don't want to interrupt the hunt. Come on, keep going!" Even in times when she herself was hurting, Becca's mom always found a way to cheer up her daughter.

Becca smiled and wiped away some of her tears. "So, Lina claims that the last gift is in this room, but it feels like a trick. Like that one Christmas where Ian put Kim's gift in seven different boxes."

"I still don't forgive you for that." Kim frowned.

Ian kissed Kim's cheek, and her harsh expression softened. Becca continued looking. She opened the bottom drawer, the last place where anything could be, to find absolutely nothing. She turned around, slightly angry she'd come up short.

"See, there's nothing in—"

Lina was in front of her, without the mask, on one knee, holding a small box with a beautiful emerald ring.

"To go with your earrings. Rebecca Bailey, will you marry me?"

Becca dropped the phone on the bed and fell to her knees, completely overcome with emotion. Lina placed the ring in her pocket and rushed over to Becca, enveloping her in her arms.

"Are you okay? What's wrong? I'm sorry, I wanted to wait until we got to Utah but—"

Becca wiped a tear away. "No, no, it's perfect. I just—I love you so much. Yes, of course, it's a yes."

Lina got to her knees and grabbed Becca, placing kisses all over her face. She pulled out the ring and gently placed it on Becca's finger.

Lina pulled back for a moment. "I wanted to give you one great memory this Christmas. I'm sorry you couldn't be with your family."

"I am still with my family."

Becca kissed Lina's forehead and pulled her into the tightest hug.

"Can we cheer now?" Ian's voice buzzed from the middle of the bed.

"Oh, sorry, guys." Becca chuckled through happy tears.

She ran over to the bed, picked up the phone, and showed her new emerald to the camera.

"I'm so happy for you, sweetheart. I know Dad would be, too."

The mere mention of her father brought him into the room. Even though he was gone, she could still feel his presence. The moment couldn't have been more perfect.

On cue, Eddie walked in and curled up in front of the couple. Becca admired how perfectly the ring fit. Lina petted Eddie's stomach while Becca cemented a new Christmas memory with her family, regardless of the miles between them.

About the Author

Jessica Daniliuk is a writer from the Boston area. She loves writing short fiction in all genres and is excited to enter the realm of YA fiction.

She is thrilled to be a part of another And You anthology. Her story "Dancing Queen" was featured in *Another Chance to Get It Right*; her story "Strawberry Macarons" appeared in *Recipes for Romance* and is available as an extended edition from Attic Ebooks; and her story "A Summer Tradition" appeared in *Just One . . .*

She wants to thank her family for giving her a plethora of amazing Christmas memories and ongoing traditions.

You can follow Jessica on Instagram at:
   @jmdaniliuk

To learn more about Jessica, visit her website at:
   jessicadaniliuk.com

Cereal Thieves

Cereal Thieves

Gwen Cole

When we got married right when we turned eighteen, people just figured I was pregnant. My mother didn't even believe me until months passed and no baby came.

We don't want kids—we can barely take care of ourselves.

But even now, I still get random texts from my mom.

"Anything new?"

But what she's really saying is, "Are you pregnant yet?" And then I hear her thinking, because she never says it, "Then why did you get married?"

No, Mom, I'm still not pregnant, and I'm probably never going to be, and we got married because we knew it was right, *and we love each other. Why is that not good enough for you?!*

As it is, I stare at my screen and try to think of a normal answer that *isn't* the rant in my head.

"What are you steaming about over there?" Jonah asks.

"My mother."

"Did she text you again?"

"Yup."

I turn off my phone and wipe my hand across the window to clear the thin layer of fog. I stare at the snow until I'm able to stop thinking about her. Then once I'm not thinking about her, I start thinking again about why we're here. "What time is it?"

I look over to see him roll his eyes because I asked him five minutes ago.

"It's 9:45."

"It's been more than two minutes," I argue.

"Apparently not."

"It's got to be. My fingers are starting to freeze off."

"Then put your gloves on."

"But they're cold, too. And it takes too long for my fingers to warm up in them."

Jonah looks at me deadpanned. "Will anything I say help you?"

"Probably not."

"Do you want a divorce?"

"Will that help my frozen fingers?"

He shrugs. "Maybe."

As we stare at each other, the inside of the truck is so quiet that we can hear Christmas music coming from a party at a house down the road.

I smile after about twenty seconds and say, "I can't take you serious in that hat."

I lean over the seat and swat the pom-pom on the top of his head. His sister made him the hat last year, and he's worn it every day since the season turned. It has blue and yellow stripes, not to mention a fluffy yellow ball at the top. It's totally ridiculous.

"You know you love it," he says, looking out the window again.

He's right, I do. There's nothing I don't love about him. We met two years ago, and a day hasn't passed without seeing each other. Saying yes when he asked me to marry him right out of high school was the easiest decision I've ever made.

While he's busy watching the house, I dig out my gloves and slip them on. Every single house on this block has Christmas lights lining the gutters and strung in the trees. The lights shine off the snow, making everything glow.

Everything is bright. Too bright.

"You're positive about this?" I ask.

"Ten o'clock." His breath is fogging up the glass, and he wipes it away with his hand for the tenth time.

A car drives by, and I watch it until it turns the corner. I tap the steering wheel, bored out of my mind, but also very, very stressed.

"Alice."

"What?"

"Stop it," he says, still looking out the window.

I throw a glare at the back of his head. Now that I think about it, this is the perfect time to bring up a certain something. He can't run away.

"So . . ." I start. "It's Christmas Eve, but our one-year anniversary is also next month."

He doesn't even flinch—not the reaction I'd been expecting. "Yeah, I guess it is. What do you want to do?"

Jonah finally looks away from the house, his expression very guarded.

"You know what I want," I say.

"We've talked about this."

"Yeah, and we still are."

"Can we do this later?"

"That's what you always say! And 'later,'" I motion quotation marks with my fingers, "becomes weeks, and those weeks become months. Don't tell me that's not true."

We hear snow crunching down the sidewalk, and a family of three walks by and shoots weird looks into the dark cab of the truck where we sit. Jonah just smiles and gives them a friendly wave.

After they're gone, I say, "You better hope none of them have a photographic memory."

"Oh, *please*."

"I'm serious."

He knows I'm right, but instead of saying so, he glances at his watch again. "All right, it's almost time."

"You better be right about this."

We wait in silence, watching the houses around us. Then it happens all at once.

The Christmas lights turn off at the same moment, and the street is only lit by the streetlamps, casting the houses all in shadow.

"See?" he says, almost giddy. "I told you they were all on a timer. This whole neighborhood is dedicated to saving electricity."

"Well that's lame," I say.

"I know, right? Let's go."

We try to close our doors quietly, but an old truck can only do so much. After glancing around at the houses, we confirm nobody is looking out their windows.

We share a grin over the bed of the truck and grab our bags from the back. We swing them over our shoulders and start up the driveway, trying not to slip where the snow is iced over. More than once, Jonah has to grab my hand to keep me from falling, and every time, I have to cover my mouth so I won't start laughing. Jonah bites his lip, trying to contain his laughter, as well.

The Gift Exchange

We make our way around to the back of the house, where a tall privacy fence shadows us from the neighboring houses. The back patio is slick with ice and snow, but Jonah kneels down despite the cold, taking off his bag and placing it gently on the ground.

With the sound of his tools making their way into the lock behind me, I keep my eyes on the houses around us. The one to our right is dark, but the one to our left is the opposite. All the lights are on, and people move past the windows.

They're oblivious to us.

An older man, who I assume is the father, has a small child on his back, bouncing around the house to the Christmas music I could hear from inside the truck. A kid a little older is following them around with a bubble gun.

"Are we clear?" Jonah asks.

I tear my eyes away. "Yeah."

A soft click of the lock and we slip inside the dark house. Almost immediately, Jonah's elbow bumps into a vase on the counter and it tips toward the ground. As he lunges forward, his shoe slips on the tile and he falls with a grunt.

"Are you all right?" I whisper.

I close the door and stand over him where he's sprawled on the floor with the vase clutched to his chest.

"All good."

"You almost broke our streak."

"Yeah, but I didn't." He stands and puts the vase back on the counter. "See? Not even a crack."

He gives me finger guns and a corny smile.

I roll my eyes, trying to force my heart to calm. The kitchen still smells like pies and sweet potatoes, like the family who lives here could pop out at any moment.

"When are they getting back?" I ask. Another question I probably ask too often.

"Next week. At least, that's what Peter said."

Our friend, Peter, works for a travel agency (I didn't even know what a travel agent *was* before we started doing this), so once in a while when he wants some extra cash, he "accidentally" passes on some information to us. We give him a cut, and everyone is happy.

Well . . . almost everyone.

These are always the easiest jobs, though.

Others are a guessing game and staked out a week prior.

I suddenly say, "Do you think the feds have one of those special names for us?"

"Huh?"

"Like, 'The Cereal Thieves,'" I say, waving my hand through the air, demonstrating a headline. "Or something way cooler."

"Like serial killers?" he asks, raising an eyebrow.

"Yeah, but obviously the kind you eat, because we like sugar for breakfast and we don't kill anyone. It's a play on words!"

He thinks about it for a moment—like he's never thought about it before—and I know I have him when he finally smiles. Because I know that smile. It only comes out when he's truly happy about something.

Getting something fun in the mail. When I agree we can order in food. When he wakes up on Sunday morning, knowing he doesn't have to go to work. It's the smile that made me realize I love him.

Jonah says in a very hopeful voice, "Maybe?"

I step closer to him. "And maybe we get so famous that next week when we're eating dinner in front of the TV, we'll suddenly hear them say, 'The Cereal Thieves strike again, leaving everyone without their favorite breakfast.'"

"That was a terrible impression."

"Horrible. But you get the point."

Jonah can't stop smiling at this point. "We've never been famous for anything before."

I press a little closer. "And nobody will know but us," I say, my voice low.

His eyes shine bright even in the dark, reflecting the light coming through the windows. Dark hair peeks out from under his blue and yellow hat.

We both drop our bags at the same moment and go for each other.

Jonah backs me against the counter, and I don't give in easily, my mouth moving with his like I can't get enough. His breath smells like the Orbit gum he chews after dinner, and his skin and lips are cold. It makes me hungry for him.

As quick as he advanced, he pulls away, giving me a daring smile. "Come along, darling, we have things to steal."

"Ah, yes. Just don't break anything."

Jonah tosses my bag over from where I dumped it on the floor and disappears down the hall, whistling the *Jurassic Park* theme song. He does it only because he knows it gets stuck in my head for days.

I shoulder my bag and go upstairs, my heart still racing a little from our quick makeout in the kitchen.

"The Cereal Thieves," I whisper to myself, unable to stop the smile that creeps up.

The only room I have to find is the master bedroom, because it's the only room that'll have any valuables. I toss my bag on the bed, but before I check the jewelry box, I go into the bathroom. It's like a hob-by—checking out the bathrooms and kitchens of the houses we steal from. It gives me ideas for my future dream house, if we ever get one.

This bathroom isn't all that great, though. The tub is too small, and the vanity doesn't even have a marble top. Just for kicks, I check out the medicine cabinet. Some people are on *way* too many medications, and sometimes I get lucky, like tonight, and find some that I can sell to college kids. I take two bottles.

Back in the bedroom, I look through the top drawers. The man has a pistol stowed away (which I don't touch) and an old watch (which I take). The woman's drawer is more exciting. She's got an envelope full of cash—probably for traceless shopping, not that I would know anything about that—and a smaller jewelry box (smaller than the one on top of the dresser) full of old rings and necklaces. By the look of them, probably handed down through the family.

These are the things I (sometimes) hate to take. I look through them for the most valuable and leave the rest. Besides, if this stuff is hidden away in a forgotten drawer, they must not care about it all that much. At least that's what I tell myself.

I toss my selections on the bed and open the big jewelry box.

Everything in there goes on the bed, along with the cash and watch. But one ring catches my eye.

I hold it up to the dim moonlight coming through the window, trying to guess its value. It had to have been an engagement ring. I leave it, knowing someone will miss something so special.

I quickly shove everything else into the bag and go back downstairs. I find Jonah in the office, clearing out a safe behind the desk.

"Hey," he says. "Find anything?"

"Yup."

I throw my bag on the desk and lean against the wall, watching him stash some cash into his own bag. Later tonight—before these things are labeled as missing—we'll go to the pawn shop and get rid of most of it. Cash isn't traceable, but jewelry can be.

Jonah closes the safe, locking it back up so nobody will know anything is missing until they open it. "You wanna go to Waffle House tonight?" he asks.

"Sure."

He straightens at that, staring at me in the dim light. "What's wrong?"

"What do you mean? Nothing's wrong."

"You just said *sure* to going to Waffle House. You never want to go to Waffle House. You didn't even want to go to Waffle House when we went a whole day without eating anything because we got stuck in that stupid airport and both share the same feelings about pricey airport food." Then he says, "Will you just tell me what's wrong?"

"You know what's wrong." That disappointed look returns, and I suddenly feel bad about asking again. "I'm sorry." I shake my head, digging my palm into my forehead. "I know I'm being stupid about this, and I know it's unpractical for our situation right now."

"Alice . . . you know we're in this together forever. You *know* that. I married you for a reason, even when everyone else had doubts about our age. I never thought I would meet the right girl. Hell, we rob houses together and have a crappy apartment in the middle of the city that we can barely afford, but I've never been happier. I love you," he says, coming up to stand really close to me.

"I love you, too," I murmur, and I really mean it.

Jonah steps back and says, "I have an early Christmas present for you."

I can't help my smile. "You couldn't wait one more day?"

"Nope, this moment is too perfect."

Then, to my utter disbelief, Jonah gets down on one knee, still wearing that *stupid* hat. For a moment, I think he's going to pull out a ring, because we could never afford to get one, and I panic a little before remembering Jonah knows me better than that. He knows a ring—engagement or otherwise—isn't on my Christmas list this year.

"Alice Elizabeth Stonewall, will you adopt a kitten with me?"

He proposed a little less than a year ago, and I never thought anything would top that question until this moment. For two whole seconds, I can't move, I can't breathe, and I replay his question until I'm sure I heard him correctly.

"*Really?*" I ask, still in disbelief.

He smiles that wonderful smile. "Really."

Then, because I can, I decide to push my luck.

"Can we get two?" I ask with big eyes. "I don't want it to be lonely when we're not home."

He gets up and kisses me, and I savor the mint lingering on his breath and the way his hands hold me closer. I keep waiting for him to change his mind and tell me all the reasons we can't have a cat for the hundredth time, but it never comes.

Then something occurs to me.

"But what about our landlord?" I ask, leaning away from him. "They have a very strict no-animals policy, as you've told me many, many times."

He rolls his eye. "We're thieves. What's one more rule broken? But—"

Jonah digs the penlight from his pocket and clicks it on. He sticks it in the corner of his mouth and starts digging through his own bag. Too soon, the night is back and my eyes readjust to the darkness. And when they do, Jonah is holding out a stack of cash.

"If all else fails, who can deny such a great bribe?" he asks.

"What if they want more than that?" I tease.

"I'll rob a bank."

"You don't own a gun."

"I'll steal one."

"No, you won't."

Jonah smiles and says, "See? This is why I married you. You know me almost better than I know myself, and you know how I can be—*me.* And yet you're still here."

We leave the house the same way we came. Nothing broken, the safe shut and locked, not a sock out of place.

Just a box of cereal missing from the shelf.

We walk down the driveway, holding hands, listening to the Christmas music the neighbors are still playing too loud. The family that we saw earlier on the sidewalk is walking by again, but this time they stop.

We've done this so many times that Jonah doesn't miss a beat. He's a better liar than I am—sometimes I'll just burst out laughing because I can't take myself seriously.

"Nice night, isn't it?" Jonah asks.

The man hesitantly says, "Yeah." Then, "How do you guys know Tom and Melissa?"

"Just friends of the family." Jonah helps me over a patch of ice, and we continue to our (stolen) truck, the family still standing behind us.

"I thought they were out of town this week," the man says. (But what he's really saying is, *They're out of town this week, what are you doing here?*)

We finally turn around, Jonah with his charming smile and goofy hat.

"We're feeding their cat while they're gone." (*We're stealing from them.*)

"I didn't know they had a cat." (*They don't.*)

"It's an indoor cat. It usually just sleeps under the bed all day." (*I just broke into their safe.*)

"Oh." (*Oh.*)

"Have a merry Christmas," Jonah says.

"Yeah, you too."

The family finally turns away and continues down the street, glancing back at us. A little ways down the street, a house has gone against the town ordinance and put their Christmas lights back on, reminding me of the holiday tomorrow.

"So . . ." I say.

"Waffle House?"

And for once, I actually agree. "Waffle House. And while we're there, we can think about cat names."

"Names, like plural?"

"I told you we're getting two."

He allows a smile and says, "Only if I get to name one."

"Deal."

We get into the truck, with Jonah behind the wheel and me next to him, and we leave that neighborhood full of large houses and family dogs, and head toward Waffle House, the pawn shop, and eventually home—a small apartment in the noisy, busy city we wouldn't trade for anything.

About the Author

Gwen Cole grew up in northern New York, moved to Virginia, and got married at eighteen after she met her husband while playing in a hardcore band. She's pretty good at video games, mediocre at skiing, and not great at softball, but still enjoys all of them. Gwen is the award-winning author of *Cold Summer*, *Ride On*, and the Wattpad five-million-reads sensation *Windswept*, all published with Sky Pony Press. She continues to write whatever is currently begging to come out.

You can follow Gwen on Instagram at:
    @GwenCole_

To learn more about Gwen, visit her website at:
    www.gwenmcole.com

One
Perfect
Gift

One Perfect Gift

Caroline Baccene

"Okay, class, you're going to write a story about a special gift you received as a child. Something that meant something to you. Everyone partner up with the person in front of or behind you to brainstorm! You've got five minutes!"

"Hey, Emma. Plans for Christmas break?"

I admit I wasn't really paying attention to Mrs. Calloway talk about the writing project, but when I finally comprehend William's words, I look up from my notebook, assuming I must have imagined hearing him talk to me. Sitting in the desk in front of me, like always during last period, is the cutest guy in school. But not like always, he's turned around and is looking right at me.

My pen clatters onto the desk, but I grab it quickly before it can tumble to the floor. Clearing my throat, I reply, "Not really. My family comes over on Christmas morning to celebrate with us and then we have lunch. Besides that, nothing exciting. You?"

"We usually go camping the week after Christmas. My mom and dad and brothers."

"Cool."

Cool? That's the best reply I can come up with? I've been wanting to have William's attention for years, but when I finally do and he tells me something personal, the best I can manage is a one-word response that is a temperature. What's wrong with me?

Thankfully, William doesn't seem to mind my reply, instead just asking, "So, what's your gift?"

"Huh?"

A small smile appears on William's face, and I swear I can almost see that amazing dimple of his that makes everyone swoon. "The gift you got when you were a kid? What are you going to write about?"

Embarrassed by my confusion, I answer quickly with the first thing that pops into my mind. "Well, one time my older cousin and I were at the grocery store, and they had this claw machine. I was really young, and I'd never done one before. My parents always said they were a waste of money and almost impossible to win. She paid the dollar or whatever and had me try it." My throat tightens slightly at the memory, but I continue, "I won this gold pocket watch. It had a horse and buggy engraved on the front. It was the most amazing thing I ever owned."

"What happened to it?"

Again, I have to hide the dryness of my throat and keep my eyes from watering as I reply, "Not sure. I guess it just got lost over time."

If he notices that I'm close to tears, he doesn't say anything. He just responds: "I had this compass when I was a kid. Brass and old. It was my dad's, I think. We would take it camping. One time when we were out by the river, I jumped in with my brothers. I'd forgotten it was in my pocket. Never saw it again."

"Bummer." Okay, now I definitely want to punch myself. The bell rings before I can think of something more interesting to say, and we file out of the classroom with Mrs. Calloway yelling behind us that our papers are due the day before winter break. One week from today. Great. I hate last-minute assignments.

"Emma, remind me again why we are at a thrift store looking for a Christmas present for a guy you've had *one* conversation with?"

My best friend, David, picks up an old bowl that even I'll admit has seen better days before sniffing it suspiciously and putting it back down. We make our way down the aisle of the only secondhand junk store in our tiny town as I reply, "It's just a nice thing to do."

"And this has nothing to do with the fact that you've had a crush on him since middle school?"

Absolutely. "Absolutely not."

David rolls his eyes, obviously not believing me before he says, "Well, I have to go. My dad is picking me up. He's taking me to the Bears' game tonight. Wanna come?"

David has been my best friend since we learned to walk, and we have a lot in common. For example, we both love dumb shark attack movies and old black-and-white movies. We hate new pop music. And neither of us has ever been in a relationship. Of course, I've been waiting for William to notice me. I'm not sure why David's never dated anyone. I don't think he'd ever have any trouble finding a girlfriend. But his interest in football despite never playing it is something I still don't understand, even at the age of sixteen. So, I give him an exasperated look and shake my head.

We say our goodbyes, and I continue looking through others' old trinkets. I'm about to give up on this whole endeavor when the light from a nearby window hits an object like a spotlight. The very object I've been looking for.

Slightly worn, made of a brass material, and when I pick it up, the needle even works still. It's exactly what I pictured when William told me about it. I quickly take it to the register, knowing William will absolutely fall in love with me after seeing this gift.

David's voice comes through my phone's speaker the next week as I'm taping the final red bow on William's gift. "It was good. A little depressing for a short story about a gift, but definitely well written and kept my attention."

"Well, I'm not sure how to make a story about my dead cousin less depressing."

When William asked what happened to the pocket watch, I couldn't come up with an answer for him. Sure, I know what happened to it. I put it in my seventeen-year-old cousin's coffin the day we buried her, a week after her car crashed into a tree on a country road just outside town when I was ten years old. A month after we'd won it in the crane machine. Was I going to explain that to the guy I've wanted to date for three years? The boy that has the cutest smile, the most intense blue eyes, and who helped me pick up the books I'd dropped on my first day of middle school? Definitely not.

Of course, David knows all of this about the watch already, since he was next to me when I put it in Olivia's hands. So, I don't have to explain anything to him. That's my favorite part of having a best friend. He just knows everything already.

"You're right. Make Mrs. Calloway weep. She deserves it for giving you an assignment due the last day of school. Who does that?"

"I know, right? Okay, present is wrapped. I'll meet you outside in five."

We hang up, and I throw the present in my bag and rush out the door to meet David at his car. Two more great things about David? He got his license, and his parents bought him a car. Sure, it's an ugly, used thing that doesn't have a reliable heater or radio, but it beats having to take the bus to school.

Staying wrapped in my coat, hat, and gloves, I shut the car door behind me as he cranks the car and backs out of the driveway. He nods to the travel mugs in the cup holders.

Taking a deep sip from the one that is always mine, purple with some weird green pattern on the front, I sigh my thanks as the warm coffee makes its way through my body, heating my throat and chest.

David turns out of our neighborhood and asks, "So, what's the gameplan?"

"Gameplan?"

"Yeah. How are you going to give William his gift? What are you going to say?"

I take another gulp of coffee before replying. "Well, I figured I'd do it at the end of class then skedaddle as fast as I can. You know, save me some embarrassment in case he laughs in my face."

David shakes his head and gives me an exasperated look. "No guy in their right mind would laugh at a girl giving him a present, Emma. Even if you were grotesque and smelled bad, which you aren't and don't."

"Gee, thanks."

"Anytime."

We pull into the parking lot of school and make our way quickly inside in a silent agreement to get out of the cold before continuing our conversation.

"You should do it now. Or at the beginning of class. Then you'll be able to see his reaction and won't have to wait until after break."

I lean a bit closer to him to be heard over the other students in the hallway. "After break is a new semester. We may not have any classes together. Then if he hates it or is weirded out that I'm giving him a present, I won't ever have to deal with it."

"But then you might never know."

"If he likes it and falls madly in love with me, surely he'll find me next semester even if we aren't in any classes together. Or he'll hit me up online. So, then I'll know."

The Gift Exchange

We get to where we separate for the day, him going left toward biology, me going right to Spanish.

I call to him as I walk away. "My plan is flawless!"

He yells back, "Coward!"

David's words echo in my head the entire last period as I bounce between staring at the back of William's blonde head and my unzipped bookbag, where I can see just the corner of my overly bright wrapping paper. Well, his one word keeps replaying in my head, because I'm definitely feeling like a coward right now. My hands are sweaty, and I haven't heard a thing Mrs. Calloway has said the entire hour. For all I know, she's telling us all how lazy we are, hating on the papers we turned in, and telling us she's going to spend her vacation in the Bahamas surrounded by a bunch of hot men. I mean, it's entirely possible.

The bell rings and everyone jumps up, eager to leave this place for two weeks. My voice is barely above a whisper as I call William's name, and a part of me wishes he wouldn't hear me. But he does, and he turns with that cute smile of his. I pull the present out of my bag and hand it to him, intending to make a quick exit but am blocked by three students leaning against their desks arguing the merits of buying collectible Pokémon cards or something.

William asks, "Should I open it now?"

"Umm, if you want. Or you could wait until Christmas or whatever." As soon as these guys move, I can get out of here. My face is on fire and must be beet-red. And it's so hard to keep from rubbing my wet palms on my jeans.

"Nah, I'll open it now." And then he does, ripping off the silver and red paper. He studies it for a minute before smiling. "So cool. It's almost just like the one I had when I was a kid."

I return his smile and nod. "Yeah, I found it in this cool shop—"

"Thanks, Ella." Then he sticks it in his pocket and walks away.

Ella. He called me *Ella.* I've known this guy since I was thirteen, and he called me Ella. He called me Emma the other day, right? Or did I just hear Emma? What in the world just happened? It's like the Earth has been flipped upside down, but gravity hasn't pulled me back to the ground yet. Have I really had a crush on someone who doesn't even know my name? Why?

My face must show something when I get to David's car, because he's not his usual chipper self as we get in and head back. It takes me a while to even realize that we don't pull into his driveway, instead ending up at Cupcakes & Cones.

"Why are we here? You hate this place."

I follow David as he gets out of his car and replies, "Ah, but you love it, and you look like you could use something you love right now. Now come on. I'm buying."

Since I've never been one to turn down free ice cream, I quickly fall into step beside him and we order extra-large cones. Me chocolate, of course, and him vanilla. Both with rainbow sprinkles.

Once we're seated at a booth and have taken bites of our ice cream, he says, "Alright. Out with it."

Slamming my head on the table but careful not to tip over my cone, I groan. "He called me Ella."

"An interesting way to pronounce Emma."

Keeping my face smushed into the table and probably collecting a lot of germs, I reply, "There's only two options."

"Hit me."

"Either he truly doesn't know my name, which is so embarrassing and makes me question why I've harbored a crush on this guy for years, or he does know my name. Although that means he intentionally called me the wrong one, just so I'd take a hint that he wasn't interested. Because surely now that I've given him a Christmas present, he must know I like him. Liked him. Whatever. Either option is mortifying."

"Is it possible he was so shocked that he misspoke? Like he had some kind of stroke or something from happiness and his words didn't come out right?"

I sit back up and eat more ice cream as I answer with a full mouth, "Doubtful."

"Then screw him. Figuratively, obviously. If he doesn't like you, why would you like him? You deserve someone way better."

"Sure, sure. I'll probably end up an old maid with ten cats."

"Cats are awesome. They eat mice and bugs, chase lasers, and did you know there's even studies that suggest cat owners have a lower chance of having heart disease? Who wouldn't want to have cats when they're old? I personally plan on having at least three."

"Fine. Cats are amazing. Forget about cats."

He gives me a mock horror face. "Impossible."

"Is that true? About cat owners and heart disease?"

"I mean, I read it on Google once, so probably."

"Tell me more about cats, oh wise soul."

"Don't mind if I do . . ."

Christmas Day arrives and my family is in super-stressed mode as we get ready for all my aunts, uncles, and cousins to arrive in full force. Well, all but one, but it still takes me a good ten minutes after everyone arrives to realize I've been glancing at the door, expecting Olivia to breeze in with a bag of her favorite white chocolate–covered pretzels and a bottle of Dr Pepper. She's on my mind more than usual this year. I blame Mrs. Calloway's paper.

The Gift Exchange

David arrives right after lunch, greeting my family with hand-shakes and hugs. I know if he weren't busy with his family this morning, he'd have been here at the crack of dawn to keep me company so I wouldn't miss Olivia. I managed fine without him but do breathe a sigh of relief when he sits next to me on the couch as my little cousins play with their presents on the carpet in front of us. It's relatively quiet in the living room, although I can hear my dad's booming laugh followed by my Uncle Hank's in the kitchen.

"Here. Merry Christmas, Em."

It's not like David and I have never exchanged gifts. We give each other birthday presents and little trinkets all the time. But we don't usually exchange Christmas gifts, although I don't really know why.

"For me? Is it a nametag so I don't embarrass myself next time I give a hot guy a present?"

"Well, it's no fun now that you know." He bumps my shoulder playfully as I pull out the tissue paper.

My hands freeze when I see inside the bag, my mind unable to process exactly what I'm seeing. Polished gold. A horse and buggy? Surely not.

Finally, my body starts working again, and I manage to pull out the pocket watch and see it glint as the light hits it.

"H-how did you—? Where did you—?"

David's voice is soft as he replies, "Found it at this antique store about an hour away. It was in pretty bad condition, but managed to get it cleaned up and working, if you can believe it. It looks pretty close to the one you used to have."

Pretty close is an understatement. It looks *exactly* like the pocket watch I won in the claw machine with Olivia. The last time I saw it was when I slid it into her cold hands six years ago, but I'm almost sure it even had the same number of horses and the cobblestone path beneath them.

"Do you like it?"

My arms are wrapped around his neck before he's finished his question, and I'm trying desperately not to cry, which is difficult when you receive the most amazing gift anyone has ever given someone. He hugs me back, and I'm filled with so much warmth, I don't know if I'll ever move. Maybe I'll find some way to fuse myself like this for the rest of my life.

I must express this somehow because David's chuckle vibrates my ear, causing tingles to run down my spine, and I'm suddenly very aware that I'm extremely close to a guy. Obviously, I've always known David is male. It's not something you miss. But for some reason, I'm just now realizing he's a *guy*. A guy who is so thoughtful and not bad looking. In fact, he's pretty great looking . . . almost hot. Is my best friend hot? Why haven't I noticed that before?

Wiping my eyes as I pull away, I'm suddenly feeling self-conscious, which isn't a feeling I'm used to around David. I mean, this is *David*.

"This is the best gift ever. Thank you, David."

"She gets my name right. At least there's that."

Even though he's teasing, my reply comes out more serious than I intend. "I'll always know your name."

I'm not sure who moves first, or maybe we move at the same time, but suddenly, our lips meet. It's only for a moment before we pull back, my dad's loud laugh echoing from the kitchen. But it's like the Earth has flipped back over and gravity has righted itself again. All from a two-second kiss. Or it could be the way we keep looking at each other for the rest of the day, stealing glances and *accidentally* brushing our hands against each other. Either way, there's one thing I'm certain about: best Christmas ever.

About the Author

Caroline Baccene is the author of the novels *Breathing in the Fog* and *A Beautiful Lily*, as well as the short stories "The Charred Grape," "When You Know, You Know," "Of Sound Mind," "A Place Called Family," and "One Perfect Gift." Caroline grew up in the middle of nowhere, South Carolina, where she developed a love of reading, writing, acting, gardening, and caring for all types of animals. She graduated from the University of South Carolina with a degree in Early Childhood Education and was a teacher for five years. She currently resides in South Carolina with her husband and son.

You can follow Caroline on Instagram at:
   @caroline_baccene

To learn more about Caroline, visit her website at:
   carolinebaccene.com

Tinsel and Tangled Hearts

Tinsel and Tangled Hearts

Amy Kelly

Kurt Cobain once said, "Wanting to be someone else is a waste of the person you are." I worshipped Nirvana, but that quote always bugged me. It felt like he didn't get what it was like to be me. All high school had been, for me, was this desperate scramble to become someone else, someone more than middling. We were all clawing for a way out of mediocrity, out of forgettable lives. When my mom died just over a year before graduation, I would've done anything to be anyone else. Even if it was just for a moment. Pretending I wasn't someone who knew that grief is just the shadow side of love—that became my favorite form of escape.

Christmas was coming again. It was her favorite holiday. Last year, the first year without her, the three of us—my father, my sister, and me—were the Ghosts of Christmas Past, and there was no way I could spend another Christmas crying. If I couldn't bring us something close to joy this year, I knew my friends would. Besides, I needed a distraction while my fate was being decided by my dad and teachesr this afternoon.

The Heritage was a stone building, one of the first in Nelson, I think, and the oldest still standing. The inside boasted decor with dark wood and wallpaper with bold prints. The walls held black-and-white portraits of people whose haunting eyes seemed to follow those who walked by. This time of year, the banisters and crown molding were alight with white twinkling lights and cedar boughs. A giant stairway ascended to the remaining hotel part, but Sarah and I were headed for the restaurant.

I don't know if two sisters have ever been more different. My little sister was artistic, loved ESPRIT, Calvin Klein, and her girl crew. She was a total pixie princess. I woke up, rolled into the nearest plaid and heavy boots on the floor, and blasted Nirvana whenever I could. Didn't stop her from stealing my clothes, though. She was petite, whereas I feel like my body type was more suited to grazing in a field. I could be cutting verbally; she was a knife-wielding spider monkey. She was wild and loud and totally unpredictable. I loved her when I wasn't a little afraid of her.

"You sure you're okay with this?" My chest tightened protectively. She was only two years younger than me, but since losing Mom, I've felt like I had to fill the Mom-sized hole in her heart.

"With what? Fries and coffee?" Sarah's eyes rolled while she pulled out her Bonne Belle Lip Smacker and applied it to her lips. "Seriously, Del. You're so intense."

"I know. It's just like . . . last Christmas was so like, tragic, and I want us to have fun this year." I caught her eyes, and she took my hand.

"Delilah, look at me." Sarah's gaze bore deeply into my soul. "We'll be fine. It's going to be okay. Besides, the only tragic thing here is your saggy-baggy elephant pants and wool coat. Eddie Vedder called and wants his wardrobe back." Her smile broadened at this. "Let's go find your loser friends."

The restaurant's giant booths and cheap coffee and fries made it the perfect hang out for a group of kids not wanting to freeze their butts on a winter day. Jen and Nathan were my solace, my family while I have been holding things together at home since Mom's accident. Nathan shared my passion for grunge, but in a rugged, lighthearted and sun-kissed way. Jen was blonde and could have modeled for Abercrombie & Fitch except she was too busy with sports. That, and we lived in rural British Columbia. Sometimes it felt like here was where culture went to die.

"So how do you think your dad is handling the meeting with your teachers? Are you still going to be grounded for skipping?" Jen asked, half shoving fries into her face and half trying not to ogle her girlfriend, Stacey. Stacey was blonde, blue-eyed, and muscular. She didn't miss a beat with our sense of humor and made Jen so happy. I was glad when she could come with us. I found her so damn cute, it made me question *things*, which I told Jen with a wink, but she didn't think it was funny.

I mentally ran an inventory of all the mistakes I kept making in class. "I should be okay, as long as dad isn't wearing his short robe." I shook my head, joking, but also all too aware of just how many days Dad couldn't get out of that robe. Grief had stolen Dad from us, too.

"You've told them about Dad's short robe? God, is nothing sacred?" Sarah said, completely dying from embarrassment.

"Don't worry. Your secret is safe with us," Nathan said. Nathan was always such a good sport with Sarah. He always gave her rides, and on the rare occasion she was with us, he always seemed to want to bring her up to speed and include her. It was like she was his little sister, too.

"Different subject," I said to the table.

"Yeah. How about . . . where is Shane?" Jen asked.

"Ooooh, I finally get to meet Shane?" Stacey asked.

"No, he is totally her Snuffleupagus," joked Jen.

"I don't get it," Sarah said.

"You know. *Sesame Street*. Big Bird always saw Snuffy, but no one else could?" Nathan chimed in.

"Oh right," Sarah said. "Sorry, I guess I'm not four anymore."

"Well, Del and Shane certainly weren't four on the bus this morning!" Nathan said.

I manically shoved fries in my mouth as Sarah said, "Ew gross, that's, like, my sister. I could die."

"Yeah, can we not talk about him? We, like, left it loose. He might have plans," I said through another mouthful of fries.

"What's everyone doing for Christmas?" Jen asked.

Sarah and I looked at each other. We both searched the other for some reassurance that this year could be different, that maybe we could bring a little of Mom back for the season instead of trying to ignore Christmas the way we did last year.

"What do you think?" I whispered only to Sarah.

"Dunno," she said. "I just don't want to be sad."

"Well, don't be then," Nathan said, taking Sarah's hands in his.

"Let's do Secret Santa," said Jen.

"Oh my god, yes! Let's ask the waiter for a pen and some paper. Nathan, I need your tuque," I said.

The waiter was actually this young guy named Bain, an old neighbor of Sarah's and mine, who was slightly handsome if you dug acid-washed jeans and butt-rock, but he was always nice to us when we came in. He seemed to have a perpetual smile on his face when we saw him working; I wondered if he thought of him and his own friends when we all sat at a table conspiring like this.

"Here you go, guys. Paper, pen, and another plate of fries on the house," he said. "Merry Christmas."

The hot, crispy, oily magic was never something I would turn down. I was so touched that I popped out of the booth and threw my arms around him, planting a big smooch on his cheek. This is, of course, the exact time Shane arrived.

Covered in snow, his eyes were saucers at the merriment he walked in on. Seriously, one would think this guy was followed by his own hair and makeup team, wind machine, and flirty soundtrack. He was so beautiful, I had a hard time making eye contact. It had taken me four years to stop myself from awkwardly backing away from him and darting into a door, a post, or another student face first upon hearing him say my name. Boobs and time made all the difference.

"Shane! Come on down!" Nathan goofed at him like he was a guest on *The Price is Right.* "You're the next contestant." Sarah moved to sit beside Nathan so the spot opened beside me for Shane.

"Finally," Jen smiled.

"You really DO exist," Stacey said. "And you are not a Muppet."

Shane's face turned quizzical, but he smiled and let it go.

There he was. In the dance of my friends—joking and laughing, and writing our names on paper, then ripping it up and throwing it in a tuque—and he just kind of fit.

His long hair was wet with melting snow and drops of cold water dotted my hand beside him before he covered it up with his. My hand thrummed with the energy of this. It permeated my whole body in a warm glow. I was my own Christmas light.

"Shane has to draw," Nathan said. "He's the only one here who isn't doing it. Wait, unless you want to?" Nathan was so good.

"Nah, maybe next time," Shane said, squeezing my hand. "I'll draw names for you, though."

He held up the tuque overdramatically, and we beat on the table in a drumroll.

"Are we keeping them secret?" Nathan asked.

"Yes!! Please! I love surprises," I said.

"You're a child," my sister said, eyes ever rolling at me.

"I am," I said. "This time of year. I can't help it. I think I might be part elf."

"An elf with moose feet," Sarah said

"Claws back, ladies," Nathan interrupted. "My delicate sensibilities."

We laughed. Even Sarah, who seldom laughed at herself, joined in. Her eyes met Nathan's in a new way, and the weird thing was that he was looking right back at her. There was nothing little-sisterly about it.

"We better go," I said, immediately receiving dagger eyes from Sarah.

"So soon?" Jen said. "We need to do more elfing!"

"Dad won't be home for another half hour," Sarah said. "Could we at least walk around town until then?"

"Yeah, Del, I'll give you both a ride home." Nathan said.

"Or I can if it's before guitar practice," Shane said.

"What if Shane drives you, and Nathan drives me?" Sarah said.

Jen and I exchanged looks. She had clearly clocked the vibe between Sarah and Nathan. Could we let this happen?

Sarah had it all figured out, I guess. The prospect of alone time with Shane felt really good, so I let go of my reluctance to have my best friend spend time with my little sister.

"Sure, let's go window-shopping first," I said.

We bundled in our mitts and scarves and tuques and bounded outside onto the lamplit streets. Each lamppost was a warm ball of light in the white canvas of falling snow. Twinkle lights ran up and down Baker Street. I loved this street in my town. Every heritage building had a window, a tribute to the nostalgia, joy, and wonder of the season.

Here, the wide Christmas window of a jewelers revealed a tiny Christmas village, dotted with snow and lampposts, complete with ice skaters and Tiny Tim riding on his Papa's shoulders. Their little lives seemed warm and splendid. Another store featured a Santa's workshop alive with animatronic toys brought to life by his magic.

Sarah found me in the group and took my hand, whispering softly in my ear.

"Wouldn't Mom have loved this?" Her smile reminded me of the one she wore the Christmas Eve we heard our dad on the roof with jingle bells.

I hugged her. Jen hugged me. Stacey hugged Jen, then Nathan, then Shane, until all of us were in a big cuddle puddle. Christmas was alive. I know people think that, as teenagers; we don't, like, believe in magic, would rather not take part in anything wondrous, but in that moment, magic ran through all of us.

Shane's parents let him drive their black VW Jetta with leather seats. I'm not sure how any kid got such a sweet deal.

The seats were cool against my damp jeans while he drove me home, but his hand rested on my knee, so I wasn't complaining.

"So, you like *Sin City*," he said.

"Oh yeah, I mean, whenever Black Cat Books has a graphic novel in. I pretty much read anything," I said.

"I get it. You're a bookworm," he smiled.

Internally, I screamed and hurled my wretched nerdy self out of his vehicle.

"Sort of, yeah. I just love getting lost in something." I tried to regain my composure.

"Yeah, I mean, I get it. Music is like that for me. Here." He pressed a button on the stereo, and the angry wails of Kurt Cobain filled the space between us.

"Nirvana?" I asked, as if I didn't worship him as the Poet Laureate of Seattle and a God in plaid. I listened to all three albums on repeat at home. My heart was bubbling with happiness; we had a band in common. I willed the familiar drive up to my house to take a little longer.

"Yeah," he said. "Half the time I can't understand what he's saying, but I, like, feel it. You know?"

"It's so bleak," I said. "Like he's an outsider looking in and doesn't like what he sees. Reminds me of this book I'm reading, *The Outsider*."

"Oh yeah," he said, still smiling. His smile could stop time.

Then the car hit a patch of ice. We slipped in circles down the hill toward my house. This slow, swirly drift, where Shane pumped the brakes and tried to steer. We bumped into an enormous pile of plowed snow and stopped.

Breathe.

"You, ok?" he asked, breathing hard.

"Yeah, uh yeah. I guess so."

I was shaky. I wondered about my poor, sweet Mom, whether her last minutes before her car hit that tree in the ravine felt like this. I needed something on Earth to ground me. I leaned over to Shane and kissed him forcefully. He kissed right back, and our hands found each other's coats and shirts, grasping for comfort.

The familiar chug of Nathan's truck, Rhoda, announced itself as it passed us, but Nathan didn't stop to check on us.

That's weird.

My body wanted to stay with Shane in the chaos of hands and lips and adrenaline, but my mind knew that I shouldn't push my first real Dad-sanctioned outing. Breaking away, I tucked my hair behind my ears.

"I better run. I think that was Sarah and Nathan who just passed," I said. "Don't want my dad to get mad at me. My sister and I were supposed to stick together."

"Do you always do what you're supposed to do?" he said, coming in for another kiss.

"No. I mean, sometimes. Don't you have guitar practice?" I asked, despite the warmth I felt begging me to stay with him.

"Yeah, I guess I better go," he said in resignation.

I had to pry my body from his car, every molecule resisting. Would I ever stop feeling such a high around him?

At least there was no damage to the car.

My feet crunched toward my driveway as I walked up to Nathan's truck.

Then I saw another love story unfolding.

As I walked up to Rhoda, broadside and around the hood, there they were: my best friend and my sister totally locking lips!

I freaked. Power-walked right into her and grabbed her by the arm.

"We better run. Don't want Dad to be angry," I said before strong-arming her away from Nathan and down the driveway.

"See, I told you she would be weird about this," she called over my shoulder.

"See you guys later," Nathan said bashfully as he got into Rhoda and drove away.

She struggled to get free of my grip on her arm. "You are such a beast."

"Really," I said, letting go. There we stood, on either side of our snow-covered deck, flakes falling on us, branches of evergreens depressed by the weight of the thick, white blankets forming on them.

"You could be with any of Dale's stupid posse, but no, you want to hook up with my best friend?" I asked, referencing the usual troop of goons she hung out with. "Come on. This is Nathan."

"Dale and his bros are a bunch of apes. You've said it yourself. Nathan is different. He's funny, and he doesn't just try to get in my pants." Sarah's eyes pricked with tears.

Now my lunch was rising into my throat. The thought of my sister and my Nathan.

"Besides, what do you care? You and Shane seem pretty hot and heavy. Unless you don't really like Shane. Maybe you're jealous?" She was almost shrill now. We stood there seething. Two dragons breathing out smoke into the winter air, sizing each other up.

"He's not just some shirt you can borrow and bring back ruined." I folded my arms. It was a low blow, but this was *my* Nathan.

"I know, Del," she said, softening. "I really care about him. I have had the biggest crush on him since he first came home with you and that stupid diorama. I just never thought he would like me back."

Now it was my turn to back down a little.

"Of course he would. Who wouldn't love you? You are like this magic pixie dream girl full of sass, with excellent style. Any guy would be lucky to have you."

"Really, Del? Does that mean you won't mind if we went out?" she said. "I really won't if it's going to hurt you. You're all I've got."

Immediately, my heart knew this to be true. Tragically true. How could I want to keep her world small to serve my petty woes over the complexity of my sister and my best friend dating? God, I could be so freaking selfish. She needed this. Even if it didn't work out. We would deal with it. We'd dealt with a lot worse together.

"Sarahbearah, he is a great dude, and frankly, I am kinda relieved you aren't getting with Dale and his friends anymore. I couldn't think of a better guy for you to be with. Honestly, sis. I want to see you happy," I said, feeling so magnanimous.

"Oh my god, lighten up," she said. "It's not like we're getting married."

The Gift Exchange

Was Soul II Soul playing, because we were "back to life, back to reality"?

"Just promise me I won't hear about your romantic life, and I will not take sides if you guys get into it." I opened the door to the house.

"Oh my god, as if."

Our Secret Santa gift exchange was planned for the end of the school week before Christmas break. I had gotten Stacey in the draw. Jen told me she had sports medals and photos in a box on her dresser. I found a vintage, painted shadow box to help display them and photos of her games. I had to be super stealthy about it and arrange it all right before the gift exchange at her place. Luckily Jen and I got there a little early so we could elf.

Her rec room had an orange shag rug, a brown floral sofa with lopsided cushions (dead springs), a coffee table that looked chewed on, and a rattan papasan chair that my sister Sarah and I sat in like two chicks in a nest. Everyone was here. Except one person. *The* person. Shiny hair, with lips I swear I could still trace the warmth of on my own. Just my luck, Shane's family took him skiing for the holidays.

Sarah and Jen both had green elf hats, complete with pointy ears. I wore my old Santa hat from Mom. Nathan, of course, had put his head through a wreath only to find out after a little while that holly bites! Stacey's mom was unreal. She had sewn a silver garland around the boat neck of a beautiful white sweater that fell off Stacey's shoulder, revealing a smooth, strong arm. The notch where her clavicles met looked like you could store change in it.

"You are stunning, lady. When are you going to dump Jen and run away with me?" I said to her, teasing flirtatiously.

Stacey smiled, rolled her eyes at me, and sat next to Jen and across from the enormous spread of food her mom had put out. Not only did her mom seem to love taking care of Stacey's friends, but I think she thought there would be twenty of us.

"Back off, lady! You wanna fight?" Jen said in mock aggression, defending her girl's honor.

"She is way out of your league," Sarah informed me.

"Thanks, sis." I said, mauling my sister and giving her a noogie through her hat.

The room was twinkling with the lights lining the perimeter of the ceiling and a single, living, tabletop Christmas tree on the entertainment unit where *A Charlie Brown Christmas* played on the TV on mute. They had a wooden balsa-wood statue with painted forest creatures on different tiers. The candles at the bottom were lit and the heat from them made the blades of the fan spin. It was something you would see at the Charles Dickens Market.

"Okay, who goes first?" I said, shoving my face full of seven-layer-dipped sausage roll.

Apparently, I hadn't timed that right, because the shocked and disgusted look on my friends' faces conveyed that they'd heard more sausage than words.

Laughter.

Sarah takes my hand in mock sincerity, "Del, this is an intervention. You are a total butt-munch." She laughed uncontrollably. Out of nowhere, she smooshed a scoop of whip cream off her trifle onto my face.

"Nice," I said, half licking, half wiping the treat off my face. "Let me try that again. Who goes first?"

"Me!" said Stacey and gave a big box to Jen.

"Hey, wait, you went over the limit," Jen said.

"Bite me. I am your girlfriend," she said. "Open it."

She opened the box. All I could really tell was that the shoes inside had the same logo as the box they came in. Also, Jen obviously loved them and gave Stacey a deep kiss on the mouth.

"Baby needs some new kicks," Stacey said.

"My turn," I said, handing Stacey my gift bag.

"Oh wow," she said as she opened the shadow box. "Wait. How did you get my stuff?"

"A little elf helped her," Jen winked.

"You are awesome." Stacey kissed Jen. "And you are awesome." She walked over and hugged me.

"So glad you are one of us," I said in our hug.

The gift exchanges went on. Jen got Nathan *Nirvana In Utero.*

"Awesome. I can replace the one I lost."

"Now me, now me," said Sarah, handing me a box.

"What the heck?" I said.

"Okay, so I know I am a bit of a butt, and I totally, like, borrow your clothes or like, let Monica borrow them. I still think it was her that put the cigarette burn in your MAUI tank. And well, I wanted to make it up to you," she said, looking at me with such stars in her eyes.

"What is it? Like detergent?" I joked.

She looked slightly pained.

"Just open it."

I did. I ripped the gold wrapping and tore open the box. Beneath the delicate tissue paper lay my gifts. Charcoal gray wool, blouses with big floral prints, tank tops and T-shirts, with lace, from the beaches of Hawaii, Mexico. There were a dozen items. This was so cool.

"So, I went to all your thrift shops and bought all the old vintage Ts, and, like, blouses old ladies probably died in, and thought maybe it would like, make up for some of the damage."

Tears pricked my eyes, and a lump formed in my throat. All those times opening my drawers to find my favorite tank top or comfiest sweater gone the way of my selfish, little resident clothes thief . . . and this gift was so thoughtful.

"Oh god, you don't like it? Oh shit, I can't take them back." Sarah's face fell.

"God no, no. I love them. It's the best present, really, Sarah," It wasn't the actual taking of the clothes that bothered me; I just never thought I mattered enough for her to ask me if she could borrow them or for her to care when they'd been ruined or notice when they were never returned.

I threw my arms around her, almost knocking us out of the chair.

"I can't believe you did all this," I said.

"Yeah, well, it was no big deal," she said.

"I guess I'm last," Nathan said.

Man, I was slow at math today. Of course, he had gotten my sister. Sarah had been a constant fixture in our group since the day at the Heritage, but they had, thankfully, had the graces to limit their public displays of affection to a minimum. Respect! You know, for my digestion.

Nathan was almost blushing. He coyly got up in his wreath, which was a massive distraction from his actual outfit: a long undershirt beneath an Oscar the Grouch T-shirt, complete with dickies and combat boots.

"Here," he said, handing Sarah a box.

Inside were the most beautiful pair of spheres on posts, red-turquoise earrings marbled with black lines. They were classic and minimal and stunning. Sarah teared up and wrapped her arms around Nathan.

She kissed him.

"Get a room," I said, sitting too close for spit to be exchanged. Ew.

"I am family now." Nathan backed away, strutting cockily, then tackled us both on the round chair. Then Jen piled on, then Stacey.

"This is nice," I said, voice strained. "But I can't breathe."

The Gift Exchange

After saying our goodbyes and thank-yous, Nathan drove Sarah and me home, only this time they paused, like, awkwardly, waiting for me to get out first.

Upon reaching the stoop inside my carport, I found a box on the step. A peek at the return label told me what it was. Wanting the anticipation of it a little longer, I ran inside and downstairs to my bedroom. By the twinkle lights of my tiny imitation tree, with Bing Crosby's version of "White Christmas" playing, I opened the box and read Shane's note. It was on the back of a postcard with an owl in glasses reading a book.

> *Merry Christmas, Del.*
>
> *This postcard reminded me of you. Anyway, I made the one thing from beach glass I found at Long Beach in Tofino. I love how it's so perfect in how not perfect it is. The next thing is because you like books.*
>
> *See ya when I'm back.*
>
> *S*

Inside was a necklace woven out of hemp string with little pieces of turquoise beach glass. It smelled like him. The book had a black cover and an ominous drawing of a man next to a stone angel statue: *The Crow* by James O'Barr. I couldn't wait to crack it.

I held the items to my chest like I was trying to squeeze his essence from them.

Life seemed to hold such richness this Christmas. My heart was so full from my friends, Shane, and Sarah. For an instant, it felt like I wasn't Delilah, the sad girl, taking care of things and missing Mom. For an instant, if I held on a little longer, I was happy. Maybe for the holidays, it would be okay to just be me.

About the Author

Amy Kelly is a former midwife, current therapist specializing in maternal mental health. Her short stories have appeared in *As the Snow Drifts*, *Recipes for Romance*, 805 lit+ art, Scribbled, Dear Human, emerge25, and Belladonna's Garden. Her nonfiction has been published in The Yummy Mummy Club and her poetry in Tiger Leaping Review. Her short story "Another Fish in the Sea," was a #1 New Release for its genre on Kindle. Amy's YA manuscript *Little Acts of Useless Rebellion* was second runner-up in the 2023 Leapfrog Global Fiction Prize. She attended The Yale Writer's Workshop 2021–2024, SFU Writers' Workshop, and was selected for the McLoughlin Gardens Artist in Residency Program 2024/2025. *Waxing Arcadia* has been longlisted for the 2025 Leapfrog Global Fiction Prize. When not writing or working, she is tending to animals on her hobby farm, enjoying her two wonderful neurodivergent teens, or making pottery. Amy's last great adventure was hiking Everest Base Camp at age forty, and she hopes publishing her books will be her next.

You can follow Amy on Instagram at:
@amykellywrites

To learn more about Amy, visit her website at:
www.amykellyauthor.com

Share
the
Love

Share the Love

Katherine Rea

Sunday, December 14, 2025

The first thing you should know about me is that I live in a town that's obsessed with Christmas. You may think that's more like the seventh or eighth thing to know about me, but trust me, it's the first. We're like the Whos down in Whoville. Except for me. I'm not exactly the Grinch, I'm just not obsessed with Christmas. And is that so terrible? You'd think it was, the way everyone acts.

Here's why I am the way I am, I think: there's this assumption that we only have happy memories around Christmas. But Christmas makes me think of Zach. Yes, he was sick a long time before Christmas, and I wasn't the biggest fan of Christmas even before he got sick. But December 2021 was when he took a turn for the worse. December 24, 2021, was the day I realized my older brother might not be coming home, ever.

The only thing that got me through that time was music. I poured everything I had into practicing my flute. Sometimes I'd play for three hours a day. Focusing on my etudes, my orchestral excerpts, practicing my technique—it transported me out of my mind in a way nothing else did. Zach had always been my biggest fan, asking me to play for him first thing when he'd come home in between treatments. After he died, I felt like I owed it to him to be the best flutist I could be. So when I played, I felt connected to him.

But now it's been a few years, and practicing doesn't get me out of my head the way it used to. I don't feel sad or mad about Zach's death anymore, or even as close to him. I just feel numb. So that's why I'm starting this journal. As hokey as it feels, a *former* friend once told me that journals reflect the deepest part of our souls. And lately, I'm afraid that my soul isn't normal; that it's not like other people's souls. Maybe it's more of a shallow pond with scummy, algae-filled water rather than a nice, deep well. Or maybe there's nothing wrong with me, but I just don't fit in here.

You see, Pine Hollow is cutesy in the way those holiday Hallmark movies are: charming downtown, snowcapped mountains in the background. But Christmas is almost like a competitive sport here. You think I'm exaggerating, but know this: One year, there were so many Christmas lights on all the houses that it overloaded the power grid. I was seven or eight at the time, and I remember that on Christmas Eve, the whole town had to celebrate by candlelight, which was actually pretty fun. People lit bonfires to stay warm. So after that, Mayor Polaff had to institute an official Christmas Lights Policy: "No one house may exceed more than 250 Christmas light bulbs, and/or 3 large or 6 medium to small lawn decorations." If you don't believe me, you can look it up in the city's official bylaws.

But anyway, back to Christmas *this* year. More specifically, Pine Hollow High's annual Secret Snowflake gift exchange. As someone who abhors tacky gifts, this week-long marathon of holiday cheer, run by our school's Spirit Squad, is the bane of my existence. And it starts tomorrow, dear Diary, with the annual gingerbread house building contest. We have all week to gift our Secret Snowflake, with reveals happening on Friday, but I'm going to get it out of the way ASAP.

My assigned Secret Snowflake is my AP Biology lab partner, Dev. I don't know him very well, so I've bought what I think is a perfectly acceptable bundle of gifts: a throw blanket (Target's brand, thank you very much), some chocolates (the cheapest I could find), and an Applebee's gift card. In any other community, that would be fine. The only problem is that I live in a place where hand-knit reindeer sweaters and intricately decorated marzipan cookies are more the norm when it comes to gift-giving. But honestly, who has the time? I went a step above the bare minimum, and I think that's enough.

Monday, December 15, 2025

Well, Diary, you'll never guess what happened to me today. I wasn't expecting my Secret Snowflake to make a huge effort. Pine Hollow is a small school. Everyone knows each other, so most people know me well enough to not go all out with a gift. But I wasn't expecting what I got.

Let me back up. It started with the gingerbread house building competition at lunch in the gym. I normally wouldn't have participated, but Dev had recruited a group of us from AP Bio, and I figured it'd give me the perfect opportunity to slip his gift into his backpack when he was distracted.

Dev said something like, "Harps, you're gonna be on our team," with all the confidence in the world. Dev has swag, I'll give him that.

I said I might skip it this year, but he was like, "Come on, it'll be fun! And how else are we gonna crush the AP Lit team, 'Crime and Confection?'"

I rolled my eyes. I hate puns. But my ears did perk up at that, because my ex-BFF, Rowan, is in AP Lit, and I knew she'd be participating in the gingerbread house challenge. I wasn't exactly mad at an opportunity to "crush" her, as Dev put it.

"Fine, you won me over," I said flatly.

And that's how I found myself at a folding table in the gym with four of my other classmates, behind a sign labeled "The Snowflake Specimens." Better than someone else's idea for our name being "The Mistletoads."

Then over the loudspeaker, Principal Holly's voice rang out: "On your mark, get set, go!"

At first, I was pretty into it. We worked well as a team: sanding the edges of the gingerbread pieces flat so they fit together without gaps, then standing them up carefully as we piped royal icing against the pieces as cement. But then I looked across the gym at "Crime and Confection." Rowan and her team were building an absurdly perfect replica of Pine Hollow High, even getting the detailing of sugar-glass windows above the gym. I glanced up at them and silently cursed myself. Why was I getting so upset at a stupid gingerbread house building competition? I don't know. But I blame Rowan. Was there anything that wouldn't go exactly her way?

The Snowflake Specimens were getting to the all-crucial part of the competition: getting the roof on. Put it on too soon, the whole thing collapses. Not soon enough, you get disqualified for not completing your house in the time limit. Trust me, I don't want to know these details about competitive gingerbread house building, but you can't grow up in Pine Hollow without absorbing them over the years.

Anyway, at this point I was over it. I just wanted to sneak Dev's present into his backpack and get to French class on time. I lied to everyone and said I needed to go to the bathroom. Luckily they were pretty absorbed in the roof. As I snuck out the side door, I could hear Dev yelling, "Get some more candy cane beams on the inside! Stabilize it, stabilize it!"

I trudged down the empty hallway to my locker. But when I spun the dial and pulled the door open, I stopped. There, dangling from the hook on the inside, was a cheap metal keychain with the word LOVE stamped across it in bubble letters. The kind you'd grab at a gas station checkout. There was a small note attached to it, written in black sharpie. The paper was ripped from the bottom of a notebook. It read, *Share the love this holiday season. From, Your Secret Snowflake.*

For a second, my mouth fell open. Cuz there's "not trying" like I was with Dev, and then there's *really* not trying. I mean, come on. The keychain probably cost three dollars, at most, and the mysterious gift-giver couldn't even bother to wrap it, or get a proper card?

And that's when I had an idea. *Share the love?* Sure I would. Absolutely. I could return all that stuff I got for Dev and splurge on that new liquid foundation I wanted instead. Perfect.

I got back to the gym just in time to see Rowan accepting the 2025 Gingerbread Trophy on behalf of Crime and Confection—a huge smile on her stupid, smug face. What a joke this whole holiday season is. I slipped the keychain and zero-effort note into Dev's backpack: the perfect re-gift. Maybe I am a Grinch after all. I can live with that.

Tuesday, December 16, 2025

Someone's either trolling me, or I'm losing my mind. It all started at the Carol-Off: the school's annual lip sync battle to different Christmas songs. I was actually feeling kinda bad about giving Dev the keychain yesterday. I was trying to blend into the crowd in the bleachers while the cheerleaders were performing their annual rendition of Mariah Carey's "All I Want for Christmas," complete with the Pine Hollow pine tree mascot flossing in the middle, when Dev popped up out of nowhere.

"Hey Harps, thanks so much for the awesome gift."

I had two thoughts: Since when was Dev so sarcastic? And how did he know it was me? "It was a joke," I stammered quickly. "It was stupid, I have something way better for you, I promise."

Dev frowned at me, confused. "It wasn't stupid, it was really thoughtful. What are you talking about?"

"Wait, what are *you* talking about?" I asked. There's no way he could be talking about the keychain.

"I'm talking about the tickets you got me for the Wild Wyomings. They're in town next month and the show is completely sold out, so I dunno how you did it."

"I . . . have my ways?"

"Their music means so much to me. How'd you even know that?"

I shrugged and thought up a lie quickly. "Your Spotify profile is public. It was pretty easy to see what you listen to most. And I overheard you talking about them once in AP Bio." As I said it, I realized how easy it would have been to find out his favorite band and try to get him a gift like those tickets.

Dev gave me a big hug. "Well, thanks again, Harper. Best Secret Snowflake present ever. I didn't know you had it in you."

My mind was spinning, trying to figure out how the heck those tickets materialized in his backpack instead of the keychain, but all I could think to ask was, "How did you know it was me?"

He flashed a grin and pulled out a note, which I scanned quickly. It said something like:

To Dev, the best lab partner I could have asked for. Thanks for bailing us out of all those dissections I botched. —Harper.

"Of course," I said faintly. Even the note was kind and personal. Everything the original gift was not.

I remember sitting and watching the next group in a daze. It was a bunch of sophomore guys doing "Last Christmas" by Wham! Even though I wanted to be by myself and contemplate how my gift got swapped—and to something *so* incredibly different—I decided to stay. I always did like that song, and the boys were surprisingly good. For a second, I thought maybe I was letting the magical spirit of Christmas touch my soul.

JK, Diary. Lunch brought me back to reality. Tuna salad that's been sitting out in the cafeteria buffet will do that to you. Sam and Alex were joking about something that had happened at marching band practice that morning, but I was only half listening. Rowan had called an emergency flute meeting, so our whole section was on the other side of the cafeteria, with Rowan handing out dot sheets for next week's football game.

That should be *me* handing out the new halftime formations to everyone. *I* should be section leader. Everyone knows I'm the better flutist. Ever since we were freshmen, Rowan and I talked about being co-section leaders. But Mr. Carmen offered her the position this fall because she was "charismatic" and "organized," and only one of us could be section leader. And did Rowan push back? Insist that we'd do it together or not at all? Nope. She folded like a cheap marching band uniform.

Yes, I'm still first chair. And yes, I should be over there in the meeting. But I'll just swing by the band room after class to pick up my sheets. If I'm not charismatic enough to be section leader, maybe I'm not charismatic enough to participate in emergency section meetings.

Anyway, enough about marching band drama. Here's the crazy part about what happened with Dev and the keychain—as if a keychain turning into concert tickets wasn't crazy enough. After lunch, while I was packing up to leave, something clattered out of my backpack onto the cafeteria floor. I picked it up, only to find the exact same keychain I'd left in Dev's backpack yesterday. LOVE, in bubble letters, just as chintzy as before, and the same little scrap of notebook paper that fluttered down to the floor with it: *Share the love this holiday season. From, Your Secret Snowflake.* Only this time, when I held it, I swear I heard the faint sound of sleighbells in the distance. It even made me turn around, but of course, nothing was there.

Either someone is playing the most elaborate prank ever, or some kind of Christmas magic is afoot. Ha! As if Christmas magic is a thing . . . right?

Wednesday, December 17, 2025

Okay, Diary, here's what I've decided: Two can play this game. I'm going to put this keychain to the test. Admittedly, my gift recipient list is pretty short. In fact, it was just Dev, with Rowan out of the picture this year. But there is one girl I used to hang out with: Zoe. I say "hang out," but it was really just our moms arranging playdates back and forth for us in elementary school, and neither of us objecting enough for them to stop. Zoe is fine—I don't have anything against her. But I'd never (normally!) give her a Christmas present. However, this holiday season is turning out to be anything but normal, so maybe it all fits.

Today is sort of a special day in the holiday marathon week. You know that book, *One Thousand Paper Cranes?* It's really depressing: a girl is dying of leukemia and then she folds one thousand paper cranes. Which, yikes. I mean, you're probably tired enough from the cancer. I know Zach was. And then on top of that, you have to fold so many paper cranes? I mean, can you say carpal tunnel?

But anyway, Pine Hollow High's take on it is one thousand snow-flakes for the children's hospital. There's a fundraiser run in conjunction with the snowflakes, and tickers for each showing how much money we've raised and how close we are to one thousand snowflakes. The white paper squares are pre-cut, so you can make a few snowflakes in between classes. They ask for a donation of $1 per snowflake, and at the end of the day, they take the money and snowflakes to the hospital.

You'd think that I'd be really into the fundraiser, what with my own brother dying from cancer, but I think that's actually why I've stayed away from it. Principal Holly asked if I'd like to be the fund-raising chairperson when I was a sophomore, a few months after Zach died. That was the last thing I wanted to do—be reminded of the hospital, or cancer in any way. Plus, it all felt so performative. I didn't want to be known as "that girl whose brother died of cancer." I just wanted to be a normal high schooler again.

All this to say that this year, Zoe is secretary of the Secret Snow-flake committee and chair of the fundraiser. In between P.E. and En-glish, I went over to the snowflake table to do my annual contribution of one snowflake and $1, and I was like, "Hey Zoe, what's up?"

Zoe was sweeping up all the little scraps of paper from the snow-flake cut-outs, and she looked really confused when she saw me. Which . . . is fair. I don't think we've spoken in at least a year.

"Hey, Harper," she said cautiously. "How are you?"

"Great, yeah," I said, holding out the hastily wrapped keychain. I'd basically crumpled up some wrapping paper around it and tied it off with green twine. "This is for you."

Zoe took it like I'd just handed her a bag of steaming dog poop. "Thanks?"

I flashed a smile. "Open it," I suggested.

"I . . ." Zoe looked back to the table, desperately looking for an escape. "I really have to get back to the snowflakes right now."

I knew, from all the playdates I'd had at her house, that Zoe and her family were polite to a fault, and no matter how awkward the situation was that I'd put her in, she felt obligated to uphold the basics in gifting etiquette—one of which is that if someone asks you to open their gift, you pretty much have to oblige.

I stood there and continued to smile until Zoe realized I wasn't going to leave until she agreed to open the present. She reluctantly set it down behind the cashbox and suggested I come back after school when the fundraiser closed, because she'd have time to open it then.

For the rest of the afternoon, it was all I could think about: Would the keychain show up as itself, or magically transform into concert tickets again?

When I came back at three, something was already amiss, because the present behind the cashbox was gloriously wrapped in forest green with lovely gold trimming.

Zoe was brushing glitter off her sleeves, chatting with one of the other volunteers when she spotted me. I could tell she was disappointed to see me, because her whole face fell, and in that moment, I questioned what I was doing.

Diary, if the keychain is somehow magic and turns into an amazing gift for someone, no matter who the recipient, shouldn't I be focusing on that? Being excited to give an amazing gift to Zoe, or whomever?

But there I was just playing a game, testing this possible magic for my own satisfaction. Maybe I really do have a scummy soul.

Ugh.

Anyway.

"I thought maybe you wouldn't show," Zoe said. She cleared her throat and took the gift from behind the cashbox. "Thank you again for thinking of me this holiday season."

"No problem," I said. "But are you sure that's the present I gave you?"

"Definitely," she nodded. "I think I'd remember if someone else came by with a gift for me today."

"It's just . . . mine was wrapped differently. And not as big. Don't you remember?"

She shrugged and gave an apologetic smile as she tore into the wrapping paper. "I had a lot going on today."

She pulled out a hand-decorated calendar with little sketches for each month and accents on the pages, and I suddenly remembered what a meticulous planner Zoe was, and how much she always loved stationery, which always seemed very old-fashioned to me. After Rowan, she's probably the most organized person I know. She gasped as she opened it, and I almost did too, just thinking about how much work it would have been to make such a thoughtful present.

"Harper! You shouldn't have! It's absolutely perfect."

A note with flawless cursive writing on thick cardstock came tumbling out from the between the pages. Again, the ripped piece of notepaper had transformed. I read it so many times over her shoulder that I remember it word-for-word:

To the most organized person I know. May you continue to use your talents to spread hope and joy. —Love, Harper

When Zoe looked up, she had a tear in her eye. "You know, Harper, I misjudged you. I thought you were a bit of a curmudgeon. But this proves you're not. Would you like to come to the hospital with me and drop off the snowflakes and check?"

Diary, come on. I couldn't say no. A curmudgeon would say no. I always thought I came off as more quirky than killjoy. So that was a bit of a rude awakening.

Before today, I hadn't been to the hospital since Zach died. Sometimes I thought about how kind the nurses had been, and that I should say hello, maybe thank them. But I always talked myself out of going. It was just easier not to.

If I'm honest, Diary, I don't want to be reminded of what happened to Zach, especially at this time of year. Mom and Dad don't talk about it, so why should I? I can go to school and practice my flute and play in the marching band and orchestra, and stay in my little bubble, because it didn't make sense that Zach got sick. It wasn't fair that he died, and that I lost my big brother. He was the most undeserving person to get cancer. And if I think about it too much, it makes me wonder why I'm still here and he's not.

But I went to the hospital with Zoe anyway, because like I said, I couldn't say no.

And actually? It wasn't *that* bad. Some of the staff remembered me, even though I wasn't sure they would. We talked about Zach a little bit. They reminded me how he was always pulling pranks on them, like hiding fake spiders under his pillow and then pretending to freak out when they came to check on him. I'd forgotten about that, and it made me laugh. Plus, it felt really cool to hand them a big check: $3,687 this year.

We hung up all the snowflakes in the ward, too, and I could see how excited the kids were to see them. It was tedious, but at the same time, I felt happy doing it. I realized I haven't felt happy like that in a while, and I miss that feeling.

Thursday, December 18, 2025

Diary, guess what? I found the keychain in my pocket when I was getting ready for school this morning. Same keychain, same crumpled note along with it. And I realized there's a really easy way for me to feel happy like I did yesterday. And that maybe that's what this keychain is doing for me, and why it keeps coming back.

It was Hot Cocoa and Pajama Day at school. Most people use this day to come in their cutest, coziest Christmas jammies: think Christmas trees and that Scandinavian reindeer design. You know the one. Also, people LOVE to match with their friends and boyfriends. I don't have to worry about matching with anyone, and anyway, I hate matching, so I wore my Halloween skeleton pajamas.

I stopped by the school to swipe a bunch of hot cocoa packets and Styrofoam cups, picked up some marshmallows from Safeway, and headed back to the hospital. One of the staff at the door recognized me from the night before, and it wasn't long before I was passing out cups of hot cocoa and marshmallows like some deranged Halloween Santa Claus. It was easy enough to commandeer a water boiler from the hot drinks station in the cafeteria. I started pushing that sucker around the children's ward, and the kids thought my skeleton pajamas were hilarious.

The whole time I was at the hospital, I thought about the keychain in my pocket and what I could do with it. Even now, the ideas keep coming:

I could give it to Mrs. Aesop. I was right on the border of a C+/B- in Trigonometry. The keychain would guarantee a thoughtful gift—one so surprising that she might err on the side of B- when it came time to tabulate final grades this semester.

Or I could give it, one by one, to each of the flutes. Maybe it would make them like me so much they'd stage a mutiny and overthrow Rowan and tell Mr. Carmen they're on strike until he makes *me* the section leader.

I could give people the most amazing gifts ever, one by one, until everyone knew me as *that* girl. That super thoughtful gift-giving girl who represented holiday spirit and the true meaning of Christmas in Pine Hollow. Maybe I'd even be crowned as a mini celebrity: the Secret Snowflake Queen. And I'd get to ride on a float in the annual Pine Hollow Light Parade. It would certainly be a welcome change from my current status as weird outcast/probable curmudgeon. But do I even want that kind of attention? Even if it was for something other than being Zach's sister?

No.

What do I even want for Christmas? Not a thing—not something the keychain, with whatever holiday magic or power or spirit it might possess, can give, anyway. I want to be section leader, obviously. But more than that, I want to be friends with my section again. I'm tired of sulking and sitting on the sidelines during our practices and get-togethers. And even more than that, I want my best friend back. I miss Rowan.

If I were going to use the keychain for anyone, it'd be for the kids in the hospital. Just tooling around the ward with the hot cocoa, a lot of memories came back. Zach was one of the older kids—just barely still considered pediatric. I remember how all the kids used to look up to him. But I also remember he cared less and less about stuff the longer he was in there. He'd laugh and say, "I don't need a Lamborghini in the garage, but it'd sure be fun to drive one."

I bet the kids in the hospital don't want *things* either. I bet that they just want to get well. I know Zach did. I can't give them that. Neither can the keychain. But I have an idea for something I can give them.

The only problem? I can't do it alone.

Friday, December 19, 2025

Well, Diary, it's the last day of Secret Snowflake week. Today's the deadline for revealing yourself to your gift recipient. But that was long done with Dev, and anyway, I have bigger fish to fry. I want to arrange a *Nutcracker* medley for the flutes to play for Zach's ward at Pine Grove General Hospital.

The Gift Exchange

I first got the idea during the Carol-Off, of all things. Sitting there, I realized how much fun it is to see songs performed live versus just streaming them. It sounds weird, but I never made the connection with my own music. I always thought of playing the flute as something that brought *me* joy, and that my sweet brother was the exception to the rule in that he liked hearing me play. Even marching band and orchestra just seemed like opportunities for *me* to play, rather than the chance to perform songs that other people might enjoy hearing.

But what if I've been entirely selfish with my music? What if I stopped thinking of playing the flute as a way to make myself feel better, and instead saw it as a way to make other people feel better? The Nutcracker is *the* quintessential Christmas classic, with loads of amazing flute parts. So what better way to spread the love?

The only hitch is that I'm going to need Rowan to rally the troops and get everyone to commit.

I squared my shoulders and walked over to Rowan's locker nonchalantly, like I used to do all the time before the whole section-leader fight ruined everything. I got there just as she was closing the door.

I took the keychain and note with me, more for moral support than anything else. Even though I didn't plan on using it again, it felt good to hold it in my hand. I wondered if the person who'd given it to me had any idea it was magical, or that it'd lead me right back to the hospital where I'd had the worst Christmas ever just four years earlier.

"Hey," I said.

"Hey yourself," Rowan said. "Missed you at the section meeting."

I shrugged. For a second, I thought maybe she was trying to scold me about it, and maybe this was a huge mistake. I squeezed the keychain a little tighter. This wasn't about me and Rowan. This was about trying to do something nice for other people. Sick kids, at that.

I pursed my lips and changed the subject. "I took your advice about starting a journal."

"That was pretty pretentious, what I said," she admitted. "The deepest part of one's soul? How cheesy."

"Well, no, I think it might have worked."

Rowan frowned in confusion. "Worked how?"

I thought about the magic keychain, which only came to me after I'd started writing.

"It's hard to explain, and I'd try, but time is of the essence and I need your help."

Rowan smiled. "Can I be honest, then, too?"

I nodded and she sighed. "You're my Secret Snowflake."

I froze. It was Rowan, then. Rowan had gifted me the keychain, suggesting that I spread the love, and it was all coming full circle now. Did she have any idea that it was magic?

But before I could say anything, she continued: "But you were so rude and shut down after I made section leader that I didn't get you anything. And I feel really bad about it. I'm glad you need my help, 'cause maybe that can be my present to you."

Was this the keychain finally working for *me*? Giving me exactly what I wanted?

I cleared my throat. "I'm not proud of the way I've handled this whole section-leader thing. I really wanted it. And I always thought we'd do it together."

"I thought it was weird how jealous you were. I figured Mr. Carmen gave the job to me as a consolation prize, since you're already first chair."

"I never thought about it like that," I admitted.

We both just stood there in silence for a moment. Then I started to smile a little. "Are you sure you didn't get me a cheap keychain for my Secret Snowflake gift?"

Rowan smiled, confused. "Yeah. That's weirdly specific. Why do you ask?"

"No reason," I said, waving it off. "It's just been a long week."

Rowan rolled her eyes. "Well, yeah. You hate Secret Snowflake Week. And most things Christmas-y."

"Used to," I corrected her. "I'm afraid you only knew the old Harper. The person standing before you is a new and changed Harper, which you'll see once I tell you what I need help with."

Rowan pulled me in for a hug. "It's nice to meet you, New Harper." Then she stepped back. "So what's your Secret Snowflake present going to be this year?"

Saturday, December 20, 2025

Last night, we stayed up making the *Nutcracker* medley arrangement, and it felt like the old days between us—before we even thought about who would make section leader, and even before Zach had gotten really sick. Maybe it was finally being friends again with Rowan, or maybe it was because I was so excited about what we were doing.

The *Nutcracker* makes me feel light in a way that no other Christmas music does. The story is all about a magical land of dolls and mice and candy. Even without the sets and ballet dancers, hearing it feels like traveling through a dreamscape. I hope that while we're playing, at least for those thirty minutes, the kids listening will be transported out of that hospital ward and into the Land of Sweets with the Nutcracker Prince and Clara.

I took the lead on the music, making sure all the harmonies were right and that each song flowed seamlessly into the next: "Overture" to "Waltz of the Snowflakes" to "Dance of the Reed Flutes," "Waltz of the Flowers," and end with "Sugar-Plum Fairy." Rowan did logistics: where we'd rent a bass flute from, coordinating schedules for everyone in the section, and then calling the hospital to get us on their schedule.

It made me remember what a good team we used to be, and for a second, I started to get bitter again, thinking how we could use that teamwork as section leaders. But if I'm honest with myself, being section leader is about organization, which Rowan is really good at and I find boring. I'd rather spend my time practicing and making music. So maybe it turned out for the best.

You know what's strange, though? The keychain disappeared. It must have fallen out of my pocket after I talked to Rowan, because when I went home after school to clean up a bit before she came over, it was gone. Maybe it went back to wherever it came from: heaven, or the North Pole—some magical, mystical land of holiday spirit and cheer. It's like it somehow knew its job was done.

I do wonder why I was chosen. Was it because I'm not Christmas-y enough? Or because my brother died? Because my own Secret Snowflake hadn't planned on getting me anything? Or because it knew I really needed to make up with my best friend? I wish I could have kept it. But maybe that's the whole point: *Share the love.* And it had to go *share the love* with some other person who needed it this holiday season.

Now, I still don't love Christmas. I don't consider myself a Christmas person, or even an especially cheery person. But at least now I'm pretty sure my soul isn't so different from everyone's here in Pine Hollow. Maybe even living in a town that loves Christmas isn't so bad—especially now that I've found a way to *share the love,* too.

About the Author

Katherine Rea is a writer from Saratoga, California. She currently lives on California's Central Coast with her husband, two children, and an orange cat. When she's not writing, she enjoys reading, spending time outside, and traveling.

You can find Katherine on Instagram at:
   @katherine_rea_writes

To learn more about Katherine, visit her website at:
   katherinerea.com

Snow People

Snow People

Lisa Freeman

I had plans to frame the invitation that was left at my front door, sealed in a violet envelope. I even took a photo of it, though that was mostly to confirm the address once I arrived. Even though I've lived in L.A. my whole life and used to frequent Century City on Saturdays with a group of ex-friends, I'd never been to Cheviot Hills, the neighborhood next door.

I straightened both sleeves and made sure the red dice cufflinks faced out. This look was inspired by a Helmut Newton photograph taken in Paris around 1975. I had never dressed this way in my life—tailored black trousers, fitted jacket, pressed white shirt, buttoned all the way up—but since I'd been outed, I might as well be myself.

The side door to the kitchen was propped open and adorned with a fancy sign and a rainbow arrow that pointed down some stairs. Another sign hung to the right of it, and written in a curly font were the words *LEAVE YOUR PHONE IN THE BASKET*. Another sign sat on a small fold-out table. It said: *WRITE YOUR NAME ON ONE OF THESE PIECES OF PAPER. FOLD IT TWICE. BRING IT WITH YOU.*

I hated following directions, but tonight it was non-negotiable.

"Hi, are you Leora?"

"Lē. L and a long accent, you know a macron, over the e."

"Hi," she said again. "I'm HP's mom. Go on down, honey." She went back to work in the kitchen, layering three large trays of lasagna at the same time. It looked like enough for an army.

"Getting ready for New Year's now," she said, taking a sip of red wine while frying sausages in a pan. The vent above the stove was on high, and as she waved the spatula at me, I could barely hear her say, "They're waiting."

It all smelled so good. I wished I had eaten something today.

I rolled my shoulders up then back and took a deep breath, relieved. In all my sixteen years, this was the first time I had ever gone solo to a party. And with her upstairs, this meant a nonalcoholic, vape-free event. I doubted there would even be gummies.

The narrow stairs creaked as I cautiously moved around potted poinsettias until I reached the bottom where a curtain of tinsel streamers separated the entrance to the basement. It was cooler down here. *Good*, I thought. *I can leave my jacket on.* My suit looked better that way. I tucked my tie into my trousers and centered my belt.

The windowless room sparkled with Christmas lights. When I

entered, it was like walking into another world. The ceiling was low, and there were tons of battery-operated candles lining the exposed pipes, wrapped in silver ribbons, and another sign held by a snowman, arms open wide and wearing the traditional scarf and black hat, said *WATCH YOUR HEAD.*

The only thing I knew for sure was everyone at this party was like me. I glanced down, looking at the rug. A snowman on a skateboard.

"Oh, don't be shy," HP said. "You're too handsome. Everyone, this is Lē."

"The one who just got outed?" someone asked me, frowning.

"That sucks," this other guy said.

"Well, I *was* wearing a Lucky Dyke T-shirt. That might not have helped."

"Weren't too subtle, were you?" HP asked, shaking his head.

I leaned in and shrugged. "I think those girls did me a favor. Wouldn't be here if they hadn't."

"Here, here!" HP gave a golf clap, his fingers into the palm of his hand. I don't think HP ever came out. He didn't need to. He was *born* HP. But tonight he looked glorious, like Pharrell Williams in a variation of an outfit the singer wore to the Met Gala. HP wore a blue baseball cap that read *Human Made,* and he had decorated the frames of his glasses with some kind of bling that looked like diamonds. Of course, he wore a pearl choker above his green velour shirt and matching pants.

This guy Justin from our school was tapping his finger on top of a soda can, nodding at me. He shared a look with HP, who gently whispered in my ear, "You're one of us now," then asked Justin, "Isn't he, darling?" HP stopped himself. "Oops. Excuse me. What are your pronouns?"

"She / they," I mumbled.

"Apologies for misgendering."

Justin gave him a side hug.

"This is my boyfriend."

And then he planted a kiss right on his lips. I'd never even seen them talk, eat lunch, or share a tray of fries. I tried not to look stunned and completely blown away. Justin was a first-year varsity volleyball god who usually wore a hoodie and flew low under the radar, but tonight he was wearing bright-red silk pajamas with white piping. HP cracked some jokes about Justin passing as straight without so much as a blink.

Then Justin said sincerely, "I'm the only one here who's not out."

"Why?" I asked.

"It's not safe for me."

HP held up one finger and said, "Yet," then put his arm around him and told me, "The only rule we have is Safety First. Especially here in the Boom Boom Room."

"Boom Boom, what?" I asked.

Justin wiggled his eyebrows up and down, and HP made a sizzle sound.

"Oops," I said. "Boom Boom. Got it."

I had just made a major *faux pas*. But Justin and HP hugged me, and I knew then nobody was going to gang up on me, talk behind my back, or make me cry. I was face to face with a new beginning, wherever it was taking me.

When Emma and Isabelle came down the stairs, I almost didn't recognize them. To most, they were your basic, super-smart, going to college in two years, already studying for their SATs types. Unremarkable. People at school called them *Twilight* because of the way their names sounded together. I used to think they were best friends, but now I wasn't too sure. Tonight they were wearing matching strapless dresses so tight they reminded me of bathing suits. Who knew they had movie-star bodies, graceful and elegant. Usually they wore super-baggy clothes. Never a hint of makeup or anything. They were like elephants who no longer grew tusks to avoid the hunt.

"Giiiiiiiirls. You're more beautiful than a couple Tiffany necklaces." HP winked then stopped and asked Justin, "Am I being sexist?"

"No, you're being clever." Justin kissed them both, cheek to cheek, and asked, "Would you like chairs this evening?"

"No, thank you," Isabelle said, studying me. "You look incredible." She led me to another part of the room.

I dipped my head and whispered, "Are you and Emma together?"

"No," she said, all flirty. "We're best buds."

The more I looked around, the more I saw. The Boom Boom Room was a work of art with hanging blue-glittered snowflakes and more snowmen, these ones made of pom-poms, and mirrored red and purple stars stuck to the walls. HP had transformed the family gym. The mats smelled clean, and the equipment was covered in snowman-patterned sheets.

The snowman thing was getting weird, though. Even the long table in front of us held a Styrofoam snowman with a carrot nose and raisin eyes that sang "Noel" and held a calligraphy sign that read *LEFT-OVERS.*

"Oh no, was I supposed to bring food?" I asked Isabelle, suddenly embarrassed.

"Nope," Isabelle said. "Do you have a gift?"

"Yeah."

"That's all you need. This," she gestured toward the grand table, "is HP's annual art presentation and buffet of what he hates. Unfortunately his family loves to cook."

There was all kinds of food, but what caught my eye were the cinnamon rolls and a platter of sliced ham with horseradish and potato salad on the side in festive snowman dishes.

"For vegans like me, this is inedible," HP exclaimed, "but the tin bucket of caramel popcorn isn't toxic."

"Yet," Justin chimed in, scooping up a few kernels and popping them in HP's mouth.

HP playfully slapped his shoulder. They were so cute together.

"And the open box of cookies has a few days left on them, if you're hungry," HP continued. "But after we exchange presents, we'll order pizza. Are you vegan? They have a pizza you can eat, if you don't do dairy."

"She's good," Isabelle said, pulling me closer. She was such a top bunk. She confessed, "HP used to put the Feast of the Seven Fishes in this exhibit, but last year it stunk so bad I told him I wouldn't come back if he did it again."

"Well, you're lucky I tossed it. This year it had an epic stink. There was a crispy fried fish that's soaked in onions, carrots, berries, and Scotch. Yeahhh. Then covered in spicy pickle sauce. And Grandpa de Luca brought some real nasty cod. Today, if it were on this table, it would make you gag."

I awkwardly bumped into a snowman piñata that dangled from the rafters, gently twisting side to side, and asked without thinking, "What's the deal with the snowmen?"

Everyone in the room said at the same time, "Snow *people*."

HP took my hand and said, "It's the theme this year. Snow people. You could say nonbinary—"

I didn't know the person he looked at, but they both nodded at each other in agreement. Most of us went to the same school. For such a small community, it was nice to see a few new faces.

"Really," HP continued, "the concept is about not letting someone else decide who you are. You know, Lē, think about it: some people, snow people for example, have no gender unless someone puts it on them. Clothing. Male or female. They don't get to choose, do they? All queers—" HP stopped again. "A nasty word that has been recycled and empowered. I'll say it again. All queers get labeled somehow, even in the gifts we're given that, shall I say, miss the beat. That's why we have this Remedial Recycling. Like the leftovers, we pass them on in celebration."

Somebody raised their cup and said, "Cheers."

"This party," Isabelle continued, "is about not accepting what others think we need. We don't have to keep someone else's perception of who we are, even if we love, or hate, them. We can be like snow people who, if they could, would make their own choices."

Ethan cleared his throat behind us. "Excuse me?"

We all turned to look.

I had known Ethan since kindergarten. He had always been teased for being finicky. He was the nervous type and had that anxiety thing. I understood the feeling, like having to look both ways before you cross the street, again and again, standing frozen on the curb before you realize there's no traffic. He was the first person I ever knew of who took antidepressants. Tonight, he wore a classic cowboy hat. It looked handsewn, the black felt embroidered around the high brim and a denim jacket, ginormous belt buckle, jeans, boots, and a red handkerchief around his neck. He was trying to look rugged, but he was still twitchy. He raised his hand as if he were in class.

HP lifted one eyebrow and paused. He could be very snappy, but not tonight. HP asked gently, "Yes, Ethan?"

"Just trying to get your attention," Ethan chirped.

"Why, darling?"

The upstairs door closed, and the sound of holiday tunes was gone. I followed HP's eyes as he looked up. We could hear someone's heels clack on the wood then stop as the tinsel parted in the middle and spread open. Beautifully dramatic. Like swirling smoke in the beginning of a Shakespearean play that changes the audience's reality from awakened to dreamland. P. Madison Santos was a sleepless night that unsettled me. Her hand rested on the banister as she posed to let us all watch her slowly take that last step into the room.

"This is Trench," she announced, patting the oversized, heavy raincoat. Then she hopped, skipped, and dipped to HP's side.

Amazing. Who names their clothing?

"Trench is my bodyguard," she continued. "I could be wearing a cheerleading uniform under this baby, and no one would even know. But I'm not." And just like that, she dropped that coat to the floor.

I sucked down the last speck of my wintergreen mint. She and I were opposites. Her hair was to her waist, long manicured nails, and rings on every finger. Tonight, she was wearing flared polka-dotted, super-wide pants that looked like a skirt, a red vest, and sleeveless white blouse that showed her toned arms. A couple of dalmatians on a leash would have gone well with this goddess's wardrobe as she sauntered by me.

"You're new."

She put her hand out, actually four fingers folded over, thumb tucked in. Was I supposed to kiss it, like meeting royalty? I took her whole hand in mine, turned it to the side, and gave it a strong shake.

HP intervened. "Princess, this is Lē."

I had always wondered what the *P* in her name stood for.

"Yeah, I know you," I said.

"You do?" She smirked, surprised.

I drew in a deep breath and tucked my hands in my pockets. *Why did I say that?*

And then, like a complete drooler, I said, "I'm bi," and shuddered.

"Everyone starts off bi," Ethan exclaimed.

"I didn't," HP countered. "Emma didn't. And neither did you, cute cowboy, did you?"

I did my best to concentrate. HP talked so fast, I had a hard time keeping up.

Princess adjusted Ethan's hat and gave a polished grin then said, "I just wanted to say welcome. I'm glad you're here, Lē." Her eyes locked on mine. I could see she wore thin eyeliner, natural looking, but the coral color on those pouty, heart-shaped lips made me jittery. I was so far out of my comfort zone I thought I was going to melt.

"Now we can exchange gifts since we're all finally here," HP hissed, joking, and escorted Princess to the circle.

"Some of us work," she said slowly. "Forgive my tardiness, everyone, on this auspicious occasion."

I'd had a crush on Princess for the last year. Just to be acknowledged by her made this party the best day of my life.

There were thirteen of us, and off to the side, a circle of pillows had been arranged on the floor. Everyone took a seat in formation, which made it clear these were assigned from last year and the year before. I didn't know where to go, but I was beginning to understand that HP was not only the host but the MC of the gay-la. He stood formally next to me and said, "Before we begin, Lē, we're going to add you to the ledger."

He saw the fear on my face and continued. "No names. Only your thumb print. To protect all in difficult times, as it says here on the front page." He opened the spiral notebook. "The only rule of our, call it a community, society, but not a club, is Safety First."

HP pressed my thumb into a pad of black ink, then directed me to press it onto the page. "You are now known as 32—like the page number," he explained after handing me an alcohol swab to clean my finger. "Every three years, this book exchanges hands."

"How is that decided?" I asked.

"It just shows up at a member's house. Like an invitation." He smiled. "Once someone found it on their bunk at camp."

Everybody in the circle told me their numbers. Princess went last. "I'm 28."

"Where are the others now?" I asked.

Princess opened her arms wide and let her fingers ripple through the air as she said, "In the world where they blend together, cohesive, safe, like a flock of small birds. Together we look larger in the open sky. Like them, we have the gift of knowing who we are."

HP did his golf clap again and said, "Poetry."

"Oh, stop it." Princess feigned modesty, fanning herself, pretending to be bashful as a pillow for me was placed between Isabelle and Ethan. I clutched my gift and walked into the circle, heart pounding. I unbuttoned my jacket, sat down, and braced my hands on my knees for whatever was coming next.

HP placed a fishbowl in the middle. Everybody put their names in and positioned their gifts in front of them, except Princess, who leaned back against a large box.

HP tossed the little squares like a salad and said, "Let me review, so we all understand how this works. We will pick one paper from the bowl, and whoever's name you pull is who you will present your gift to. As we've seen in previous years, sometimes these gifts are downright awful. Unfortunately, cruelty is part of our history or herstory. We don't excuse it, but we don't stop the rest of our lives to stare at it either. Tonight we pass this stuff on with good cheer and tell a story about the person who gave the gift, even if it's a memory from long ago."

I didn't know we were going to have to talk. I felt a twinge at the base of my spine.

"As your host," HP sighed, "I will start the circle. And since we're an odd number this year, I will also deal with that toward the end." He reached into the bowl, jiggling it a bit, then used two fingers like tongs, pulling out the first folded piece of paper, opening it like someone was pouring ice water over his head, and said, "Justin?"

"Did you plan this?" Princess asked.

"We did not," HP said sternly.

Justin reached for the gift. HP hesitated then placed it in his hands as a car alarm went off on the street.

Ethan smiled. "Ominous."

We watched Justin untie the bow and put it in his hair, looking at me. He said, "Waste nothing of a gift," then opened the container and looked inside, stunned, as he pulled out something so small it fit into his palm.

His voice crunched like dry leaves. "I gave you this!"

HP looked at it, then at Justin, who didn't blink as his gaze turned into a stare. He was holding a blue rabbit's foot, small nails still intact on the tiny paw that dangled from a chain.

The room tanked into a hush, a silence so tense the air got sucked out.

"Why?" Justin looked up.

"Because I don't eat anything with a face? I'm vegan, a lifelong member of PETA, and all our dogs are rescued," HP spewed sharply.

"It was a joke."

"At the expense of an innocent animal. I give it, ironically, back to you, my boyfriend, the love of my life. Despite your pathetic attempt at humor, I adore you, and I want you to know, although I hate the gift, I love you. All the risks you take for us to be together and how you insist upon teaching me volleyball, which I will never be any good at."

Then they started singing the same Billie Eilish song about love, out of tune with each other. And before Justin put his hand in the bowl, he put his arm around HP and kissed him. I'd never seen two boys kiss like that in person.

Justin read the next name of the next person who then gave a gift to the next person, and so on. All kinds of gifts and all kinds of stories. An *Avatar* DVD set and a story about the annoying cousin that said, "I see you," just like they do in the film. Somebody's parents gave them a membership to Mornings with Mozart on the classical station. And this girl with wide-set blue eyes dumped her gift, a grocery bag of vitamin packs, all over the floor. Princess claimed all the A's. Seems she loves retinol for her skin. But the funniest one was the *Titanic* LEGO set given to Emma, who rattled on about being dyslexic.

"It could have been worse," Isabelle said. "I've seen a seven-thousand-piece one of the Millennium Falcon. You know how long that would take to put together?"

"That is the thing about my aunt," Emma said. "She would have loved sitting at the table with me for the next two weeks building it. She listens. Always has. And I love her for that."

Some of the gifts were not disguised well. Like the one Ethan gave a guy named Oliver with shoulder-length red hair. This was the heart-stopper of the exchange, no pun intended. It was obviously a book.

HP demanded, "Who gave you that? I mean, Ethan, you're never going to take a bath in a cold stream, live in a trailer, run a ranch, or herd sheep, are you?"

Princess continued, "Or live alone in a pain so deep you just keep falling . . ."

"Maybe he wants to eat beans over an open fire, peel potatoes," Isabelle said.

HP stomped his foot. "Will you stop, please. Let him tell us."

Ethan started sweating so much it looked like he had stepped out into a torrential rain. Everyone took the moment in stride and waited until he finally said, "I still haven't learned to ride, but my little sister knows I dream of having horses someday. She found this copy of *Brokeback Mountain* at a garage sale, so excited to hear it was about gay cowboys, and bought it with her own money. But she never read it. She didn't know this story is my greatest fear. Maybe all of ours. That we would live in pain instead of love."

I watched Princess's eyes start to tear as she said, "I'd like to nominate this for the Best Worst Gift." When everyone applauded, I discreetly pulled out my pocket square and passed it to Princess to dab her tear before it fell.

"How gallant," she whispered across the circle to me. "Thank you."

Oliver balanced the book on his head. "I'll carry this gift for you."

Most people were soft-spoken when they talked about their gift-giver, but some were downright hilarious, unbelievably funny, unapologetic. They were sharp-edged with an arsenal of one-liners. I couldn't remember the last time I felt this good or laughed so hard. And then, HP called my name.

"Wait. I don't understand."

"Remember, we're an odd number this year. Because there are three people left," he said, "I choose the next gift-giver and then that person will choose the next gift receiver, and the last person—" He gave a theatrical pause. "Gets to choose who they give the last gift to."

My face heated up, and I put an icy can of ginger ale against my neck, trying to play it cool. *Please don't let me pull her name, please don't let me pull her name.*

Then I unceremoniously yanked out a piece of paper. *Oh fuck*, I thought and shot a look in Princess's direction. My stomach sank, and I said her name for the first time. "Princess."

I got up and placed the gift before her. She offered the corner of her pillow and said, "Sit."

The Gift Exchange

I wanted to apologize before she opened it but said nothing. It was a bit late for regret. As Princess removed the layers of wrapping, my pulse quickened. She thumbed inside the scented tissue paper and leaned back, looking at the gift, then at me, then back to the gift, and said, "So beautiful," holding up the lacy underwear, the bra to match, and inhaling the potpourri sachet like it was a drug. She closed her eyes, clutching the underwear under her chin.

It was my turn to talk.

"My grandmother gave me them. Inappropriate, don't you think? Grandma's desperate. I think this was her last attempt to make me a lady who wears this kind of stuff."

"Which you are not, dear butch." Princess batted her eyes.

"Never will be."

Princess kissed the underwear.

"If they don't fit, there's a gift return."

I covered my face thinking about Princess trying these on, and then she held them up to examine them. The lace. The flowers. The mauve. The horror.

"No, these look like they'll fit. Tell us about your grandmother."

"She's had a lot of work. I mean, she looks fifty, but she's a perky eighty-nine, you know."

"These are very expensive. I won't be losing them."

"Well, my grandma is funny. That's what I love about her."

"Humor is a great defense mechanism, isn't it?" Princess asked, still holding the underwear like it was gold.

"She used to give me bows, petticoats, and dolls."

"What did you do when you received these?" Princess asked.

"I said thank you."

"Well, it *was* Christmas," she continued.

"Nope. It was the last night of Hanukkah."

"I see. Why didn't you say anything?"

"She doesn't understand . . . snow people."

"Ah." Everyone nodded.

"I mean, when I started getting piercings, she yelled at me. Because I couldn't be buried next to my grandpa at Mount Sinai Cemetery. She thinks the body is a temple."

When I stopped, Princess gently put the panties down and took my hand. Hers was bigger than mine, warmer and softer. "Go on."

"Like I said, my grandpa was buried at Mount Sinai, you know that big cemetery under the airport? And when his casket was being lowered into the ground, my grandma put her arm through mine. She wanted me close to her. When I asked her why, she said, 'I was hoping you'd crack a joke. And because you're my favorite. I love you more than any *faygele* I've ever met.'"

"What is a *faygele*?" somebody asked.

"It's Yiddish for . . ." I cleared my throat. "Well, not a nice word for gay. You know." I looked around the room to find a few knowing nods. "It was so wrong. But . . . she was right. It was right. What she said. How we are together. But then she gave me this gift, so I don't know about her." I didn't like being the center of attention. "Your turn, Princess."

"Can't make this up." She pulled my name.

Princess tried to lift the heavy box.

I said, "Let me help you. What's in here?"

"You tell us," HP said. "She dropped it off yesterday and made me promise not to go near it. Left it right there under the stairs."

Princess's creamy skin began to flush as she held her wrist then folded her hands back into her lap and made a loud sigh, twisting the ring on her pinky and slightly turning away, watching me out of the corner of her eye then looking around at all of us before her hair fell over the side of her face like a curtain.

She scoffed and said, "The opening is always nerve-racking," pulled a feather from a slit in the pillow, and daintily blew it upward as if she were amusing herself while waiting for the bus.

Someone handed me scissors as Princess cleared her throat, acting suddenly as if being on display was not her most favorite thing in the world. I decided to kneel instead of bend over the large box. I didn't want to look weak, and if I squatted, well, there'd be no repose.

I started pulling out the bubble wrap. Princess was watching my every move, sinking back a bit as I asked, "Can I reach in? Does it bite?"

"No, but I do. Haha, just kidding. My brother gave it to me."

As soon as I touched it, I knew what it was and used both hands to pull out the bright pink bowling ball.

"Thank you," I said to Princess. "What's the story?" I tossed it up in the air and caught it. "This is better than my weights. But there's something written. What's it say?"

I read the word painted by the finger holes. *Bakla*.

"It's Filipino," she said. "Not a nice word. Kind of like *faygele*," she tried to joke. "On the card with it, my brother wrote I 'needed to get some balls. Here's one.'"

The room went silent as we understood how cruel this gift was becoming.

"This could win the Worst Gift," Justin said.

"I thought it would be the rabbit's foot," Emma continued. "But I might be wrong."

Princess sat up stoically. "As for bowling, before my brother was the meanest, ugliest person I've come to know, we used to go bowling every Saturday. Everyone here knows we competed as a team. We took the bus to Santa Monica Lanes on Pico. It's torn down now, but it used to be the best place in the world. Tons of birthday parties, one after another. Sometimes we were given cake. And once or twice our lane and shoe rentals got put on someone else's tab."

There was silence again until Princess said, "What makes me the saddest is he always knew I was a girl. When we were young it didn't bother him. Then he started taking it personally."

All I could focus on was Princess's hand trembling in mine. I didn't pay attention to the last gift given, but when everybody applauded and it was over, I couldn't wait for the pizza. I was starving and went to peruse the buffet. Princess and I reached for the last cookie at the same time. Our hands touched again.

"Excuse me. You have it," I said.

My heart was like a hot-air balloon going up up up.

"No, let's share," Princess countered, breaking the sugar cookie in half. "Come over here," she said, wandering off. "I need a fresh soda."

We walked to the far corner of the basement where there was a couch. Next to it were suitcases stacked, boxed water bottles, a plastic bin of canned food, and flashlights. The earthquake kits.

"Now I know where to come after the big one." Princess giggled.

The lights were dimmed back here, and the small refrigerator hummed loudly. But before she got her drink, she stopped and sat on the arm of the couch and looked me over.

"Maybe we should do this standing."

"Do what?" I steadied myself and held her gaze.

Princess leaned in a bit and asked, "Do I have any crumbs on my face?"

I dusted off the side of her mouth. "Just a speck."

"When I graduate, I'm going to Singapore to get a job as an au pair, then it's off to the Philippines to enhance my beauty." She tapped her Adam's apple. "I might not come back. You know, Ethan isn't the only one with dreams. Someday I want to get a text that reads: *Woke up thinking about you.* I want a man that makes me feel loved."

"So you're into guys?"

Princess gestured. "Depends. I've never had a lesbian boyfriend before."

I didn't know what to say to that, so I said nothing.

"What's wrong?"

"I feel like an imposter."

"Why?"

"I've never kissed a girl. What if I don't belong here with the snow people?"

She folded her arms and pretended to look serious. "What are we going to do about that?" When I didn't answer she continued. "The kiss thing."

A mini movie began to play in my head where time slips away, and everything moves agonizingly slow until it stops. It felt like a door was opening to two rooms I didn't know were connected. I was frightened to look inside but also compelled to. Her lips parted. I could smell Darlington tea from hours before, the cinnamon in the cookie, and the word *yes* lingering, shimmering in front of me. I lifted my chin. She put her face close to my ear and waited.

One of my hands slipped around her waist, the other scooped the back of her neck. "I want to give you something." Then I paused as I rose to my tippy toes, looked her in the eyes before I closed mine, and kissed her.

Soon our tongues were so deep in each other's mouths I could taste her childhood and see my future, layered in shades of apricot. The best gift ever came as a surprise. It cost nothing and would last forever.

About the Author

As an actor, Lisa Freeman was in films such as *Back to the Future I* and *II* and *Mr. Mom*, which led to her career in writing. Her creative pursuits focus on the LGBTQI community. She has an MFA in Fiction and Pedagogy in the Art of Writing. Sky Pony Press published Lisa's young adult novels, *Honey Girl* and *Riptide Summer*, the first two installments in the Sisters of Sand series, which blends historical fiction with surf mythology, captivating readers of all ages. The only thing straight about Lisa is her hair. She shares her life with Phranc, her partner of twenty-nine years, and their children.

You can find Lisa on Instagram at:
@lisafreemanauthor

To learn more about Lisa, visit her website at:
www.lisa-freeman.com

Contributors' Library

Please also look for these titles, which were written by, published by, or feature the authors in this anthology.

Note that some may not be YA titles.

A Beautiful Lily
Caroline Baccene

Breathing in the Fog
Caroline Baccene

The Charred Grape
Caroline Baccene

A Serendipitous Summer
includes "First Time?"
Caroline Baccene

Cold Summer
Gwen Cole

Ride On
Gwen Cole

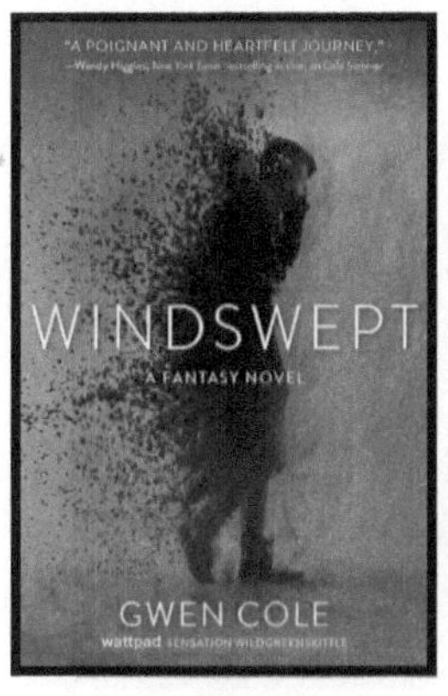

Windswept
Gwen Cole

All Year with Anthony
Katie Fitzgerald

Coming Back to Christmas
Katie Fitzgerald

Perfect on Paper
Katie Fitzgerald

Honey Girl
Lisa Freeman

Riptide Summer
Lisa Freeman

12 Knights of Christmas
includes "Someplace Like
Home for the Holidays"
Justine Gunn

Strawberry Macarons
Jessica Daniliuk

Another Fish in the Sea
Amy Kelly

Prairie Tale
Amy Kelly

Dark Days
Kate Ormand

The Wanderers
Kate Ormand

The Pack
Kate Ormand

Seeking Sanctuary
Desi Stowe

Done
Desi Stowe

Shadows
Desi Stowe

Red Gate by the Bridge
Desi Stowe

About the Editor

Nicole Frail has been a professional editor of fiction and nonfiction books for adults and children since 2009. Between 2012 and 2024, she worked as an acquisitions and project editor for a traditional publisher based in New York City while simultaneously working with independent/self-publishing authors via her small business, Nicole Frail Edits.

In mid-2024, Nicole switched gears and decided to take her "side gig" full time, expanding the services offered through Nicole Frail Edits, LLC. Shortly after, she formed her own small press, Nicole Frail Books, LLC, to publish anthologies born out of short story contests as well as ebooks and other projects still to come. NFB now has three imprints: And You Press, Attic Ebooks, and InkBridge Books.

Nicole lives just outside Scranton, Pennsylvania, with her husband, three little boys, and two Tuxedo cats.

You can find Nicole Frail on Instagram, Facebook & Bluesky as:
@nicolefrailedits & @nicolefrailbooks

And visit her websites at:
www.nicolefrailedits.com
www.nicolefrailbooks.com

Acknowledgments

Thank you to the following for all of the support, trust, and excitement they've shown me and my little press throughout this process.

To ALL of the authors who submitted to the short story contest, thank you for finding the prompt enticing enough to want to write about and for sharing your enthusiasm for it!

To the authors featured in the anthology, thank you for working on (yet another) quick schedule and for lifting each other up during the process.

To Stephanie Dunlap, a Fall 2025 student intern, who has been right by my side for this book from first edit to last, you continue to impress me! I hope you're as proud of this little book as I am.

To Happily Booked PR for managing our ARC team for this book. I hope I didn't push you too close to your limits! ;)

To the NFB Street Team, for being adaptable, enthusiastic, supportive, and overall awesome. We're growing, little by little, and I appreciate you all.

To the local NEPA readers who continually show up at craft fairs and vendor events and are eager to get their hands on these anthologies: you make my day every time you stop by to say hi and see what's new. *heart hands*

And, as always, I'm forever grateful for my guys: Matthew, Cooper, Travis, and Eli.

&You

Another Chance to Get It Right: A New Year's Eve Anthology
9 Stories

As the Snow Drifts A Cozy Winter Anthology
9 Stories

Craving You A Spicy Valentine's Day Anthology
12 Stories

Recipes for Romance A Sweet Valentine's Day Anthology
19 Stories

Anthologies

**Just One
A Summer Romance
Anthology**
12 Stories

**Not As It Seems
A Gothic
Anthology**
17 Stories

**The Gift Exchange: A
Young Adult Holiday
Anthology**
10 Stories

**Home for the Holidays:
A Christmastime
Anthology**
12 Stories

And You Press, or &You Press,
is an imprint of Nicole Frail Books, LLC,
an independent ("indie") publishing
company located in Avoca, Pennsylvania.

And You Press was created to release the anthologies built from the short story contests that launched NFB in the fall of 2024. The name reflects the requirement that every book published under this imprint will have multiple collaborators so that every title released brings multiple voices to each project.

These titles may be additional anthologies, novels with two or more authors, author and illustrator teams, or something else entirely. As long as the work has multiple creators who will be credited equally for the work they've put into it or will put into it, it may be appropriate for this imprint.

To learn more about submitting a query to And You Press, visit www.andyoupress.com.

Readers!
Join the NFB Street Team for exclusive first reads and swag from And You Press!
www.nicolefrailbooks.com/street